# *First Person Singular Vol. 2*

## 85 Very Short Stories of Wit & Wisdom

## Ross Ulysses Munroe

Manor House

## Library and Archives Canada
## Cataloguing in Publication

Title: First person singular / Ross Ulysses Munroe.
Names: Munroe, Ross Ulysses, author.
Description: Content: Vol. 2. 85 very short stories of wit
& wisdom
Identifiers: Canadiana 20190239891 |

ISBN 9781988058641 (v. 2 ; softcover) |

ISBN 9781988058658 (v. 2 ; hardcover)
Classification: LCC PS8641.L97 F57 2019 | DDC
C813/.6—dc23

Cover Design-layout / Interior- layout: Michael Davie
Cover art: Oneinchpunch / Shutterstock
Edited by Virginia Munroe
First Edition

144 pages / 27,200 words.
 All rights reserved.
Published November 2020
Copyright 2020
Manor House Publishing Inc.
452 Cottingham Crescent, Ancaster, ON, L9G 3V6
www.manor-house-publishing.com   (905) 648-4797

Funded by the Government of Canada |  Canada

*For Arielle Munroe Boyes,*
*gifted to the world by Mackenzie & Dallas*

# Introduction

When I was 18, I went to my friend Jocko's Century cottage on an island in the Kawartha Lakes for a weekend getaway with buddies.

The majesty of Nature abounded, and I had an epiphany sitting on the dock with the lake all around.

The wind had riffled the water with a thousand dancing maidens, glistening in the waning sun.

Looking closer, a scene began to develop in every wavelet, each individually telling its own story and together, forming a grand tapestry of a unified whole.

Such is the manner in which my life has played out since. And this experience has set the tone for the pages that follow, both the sublime and the mundane.

# Table of Contents

## The Book of Ancestors  - 117

## The Book of Spirit  - 127

## Reader Endorsements:

*'A tour de force!'*
Susan Gerovsky

*'Beautiful writing in stories well told...'*
Lisa Bostock

*'Beautifully written!'*
Ann Urban

*'Great short stories! Ross is one of the best around!'*
Mitch Gold

*'I love the stories, Ross, and they're beautifully written!'*
Fern Levitt

*'Delightful, masterful storytelling!'*
Karim Mirshahi

*'AWESOME!'*
Jocko Crerar

*'Beautiful work!'*
Maria Ricossa

*'Very visual writing...'*
Tom Fiore

*'I love this... Thanks for the journey, Ross!'*
Kenneth John McGregor

# About the Author

Ross Ulysses Munroe is an award-winning creative talent, having served as Executive Editor and writer of a number of periodicals with his wife Virginia, a children's book, various screenplays and short stories and more.

He also produces and directs story-driven jazz videos and has received special recognition at the acclaimed NXNE Film Festival. Ross is known for his humour and incisive perspective on the human condition.

Ross' latest work is showcased in Volume 2 of his series, ***First Person Singular*** — a collection of short stories, essays and insights certain to provoke and entertain.

From the sordid to the sublime, Ross' writing is primarily drawn from his personal experience, in a delightful and unconventional mix of irony and pathos.

# The Book of Life

## Rigged

It's thirty below zero as the sun readies to rise on the
dawn of man.

I am on the rig floor,
this subzero ice covered saw-tooth monster
where I stand like a sacrificial fool
in a gargantuan one-sided struggle of steel and sinew
and oil and blood
ripped down to the bone but unbowed
the metal and mettle in a fusion
where the piercing shards of life flay flesh and fat
clawing away the living veil
until it begins to tease the light beyond its ability to
resist
turning the night into the truth of a time before
yawning to consume the soul of all that is edible
not leaving even a scrap
running me down into the bowels
of all of it from where it issues forth
and into the world.

In this place, in this time, the eye never blinks
because the mind never closes.

## The Human Beings

When I worked in the bush, we would hit town every once in a while.

The fond memories of the crew quaffing whiskey by the quart all night, the beating of chests, the fistfights around every corner, in the streets and in the hills, the adulterous cavorting of short-lived townsfolk and grand tales of improbable heroics on the rodeo circuit are with me still.

There was one place, however, the old hands warned against ever going, despite their adventurous spirits. 'Never go to the Indian bar. They despise us and they will tear you limb from limb!'

Looking around at the current company I was keeping impelled me immediately to go there. After all, what could be worse?

When I walked up to the bar, the dozen or so Cree hanging around the door looked at me like I was a ghost. I had the feeling I might become one in short order. But they parted and let me pass as some sort of oddity.

I opened the door and I was confronted by two hundred and fifty inebriated tribal members, wrestling in drunken extreme slow motion, wobbling unsteadily, falling onto the wooden floor and sweeping their women off their feet on the way down.

Meanwhile, the band on stage stumbled through its repertoire, to the rapture of absolutely nobody.
I sat down at a table and ordered a beer. After a few minutes, a few of the tribe stopped and looked at me, blinking slowly. Then they went back to the matter at hand.

I think they knew I had no animus or any preconceptions, so they left me to myself, a ghost among Human Beings.

But once I got settled in to watch, a vision appeared to me. Above them all was an Eagle, soaring, ever-watchful, unruffled in its majesty. I felt an unbounded sense of honor, of grandeur, of ancient wisdom, emanating from this embodiment of the people, despite their current condition — one so clearly absent in the roughnecks across town.

That night I had a dream.

I am the Eagle itself, circling in the wide open sky above a village, witnessing without malice nor forethought, as my brethren are being massacred by Federal troops in battle order — men, women and children all slaughtered in twos and threes, until every stricken soul is liberated and rises to join the great dance in the sky.

The heart of the Earth grows a little heavier with weariness at the travesty. But the spirit of Heaven rejoices at the homecoming. And I am at peace.

# How I Invented the Frisbee

Please don't tell anybody, I was only seven years old.
But I was lonely a lot at that age, and always looking
for a little distraction.

We lived in the top two floors of an old Victorian
mansion near the University of Toronto, and my
bedroom was on the top floor.

One day, I discovered that I could climb out on the
slate rooftop and nestle into the corner, looking down
at all the other kids in the neighborhood.

At night, it was particularly magical, the lights of the
city silhouetting the rooflines of the adjacent houses
against the night sky, something out of an urban
fairytale.

But soon I became impatient and went looking for
other things to do. My parents were out one evening,
and I came across my father's 78 jazz records. They
looked like flying saucers, so I decided to give them
a whirl.

I grabbed a handful and climbed out the window and
onto the slate tiles.

I took careful aim at nowhere in particular, wound up and fired one at escape velocity. It arced gracefully through the air, crashing on a roof two or three houses down the street, the brittle shellac resin exploding on impact into a shower of little pieces, with accompanying sound effects.

It was thrilling. I launched a few more with the same result, trying different grips and twisting techniques, until my youthful conscience got the better of me.

Forward spin. Backspin. Sideways wobble. Vertical twist. End over end. Even a discus throw.

Little did I realize that these precious Jazz albums had been meticulously sought out and archived. I was the one to suffer later in life for my sins, for I now have that same collection in my grateful hands, missing a few of them, of course.

Suddenly, I heard my parents coming home and I scrambled back through the window and into bed, closing my eyes just in time for them to look in on me.

'He looks so angelic, when he's asleep,' my mother said, my father nodding in assent.

Which was very fitting, because while they were out, I had been to the stars and back.

## To an Ad Agency in Europe

Dearest Eugene:

Okay, got the briefing info on the project.

I'm not doing this until Sun. a.m. my time, because I have to mull it over, consider it carefully, strategize the approach, preconceive the ideation, conduct an inner blue-sky session, sit in a cold bath with ice cubes arguing in the hand mirror to get the proper motivation, pull out what's left of my hair, agonizing — while adding to the billings — yet still continuing to think about fingernails on a chalkboard, razorblades in apples, red ants attacking black ant colonies & carrying off their eggs, subsequently throwing dumptrucks full of crumpled paper into the trash & setting them on fire, then a break while the fire dept. arrives, that sort of thing.

I'll then throw jelly at the wall to see what sticks, and run it up the flagpole to determine which way the wind is blowing. Then, finally, I will be able to put it on paper. In invisible ink, without the decoding chemical. Only at that point, will it finally become real and I will have Made It So and forward the result.

Please send a 50% deposit, so I can get started. No rubles this time, plse.

Yours, as ever,
Ross

# Art with a Capital F

A friend of the family was a Sanitary Engineer. He never went to university, and all he ever got was the Third Degree, but he took pride in his urban beautification work.

Now it just so happened that the City was celebrating Art in the Park, and creators were out in force erecting their 3-dimensional abstractions in preparation for the great unveiling on the weekend.

Promotion of the event was heavy, and everybody was invited: the public, the press, the local councilor and especially the tourists. But nobody told our friend. He was almost fired from a good Union job as a consequence.

It seems he was driving around his route with his crew early in the morning before the show, and came upon the abstract installations.

'How was I supposed to know it was art?' he lamented later. 'It looked like a pile of garbage to me!'

With that they all pitched in, pitched the art into the truck, and drove it off to the dump. The Festival was, unfortunately, cancelled.

## The Cannibal & The Rabbit Runs

I don't know how Wally came to the commune, but at sixty, he was three times older than the rest of us. He told good stories, though, so we told him he could stay as long as he always paid his rent.

He'd tell us about his life in the bush, hunting deer and trapping rabbits. Or his friend, Martin Hartwell, whose plane crashed in the Arctic, leaving him with dead passengers and broken legs.

Needless to say, Hartwell couldn't walk out and his radio was toast, so over the next days he became very hungry indeed.

Up hard against his impending doom, he began nibbling on his fellows and soon was having his friends for dinner on a regular basis. When he was finally rescued, he greeted his rescuers by saying: 'Welcome to the camp of a cannibal.'

Wally's story was so spellbinding, we forgot to ask for the rent. Then he would disappear for days and reemerge presumably from some encounter with a grizzly or worse. After a while, we caught on. He had no money and never would.

To help Wally out we made a deal. I handed him some guitar strings and told him he could stay if he snared some rabbits for the household.

The wire slips into the eyelet at the end and is perfect for hiding over a rabbit run. 'I know just the place,' he chortled. 'I'll be back in three days!'

A man of his word, Wally came in three days later and to our amazement, pulled three rabbits out of his knapsack as if by magic.

'I'll make some stew,' I said and began preparing a hearty meal, while Wally recounted his adventure. That's when I noticed something strange.

'Wally,' I said with a grin. 'Did you snare these rabbits in the Farmers Market?' Sure enough the rabbits were skinned and headless, with a Farmers Market label on the side.

We never saw Wally after that, but we were sure he was in the middle of telling a good story to somebody somewhere.

# Damned If You Don't

There is a beautiful church in Germany dating back to the early 1600s that rises with spires nigh into Heaven, nestled in a storybook town that evokes the spirits of an earlier time, when life was simple and all was well with the world.

The townsfolk enjoyed the peace of mind imbued by living under the protection and blessing of the Most High and Holy.

The building itself is adorned with exquisite works created by the finest artisans of the Age and relics too, fingers and noses of great value are here and there, take your pick. Almost nothing seems to have been changed in hundreds of years and the stones themselves seem to converse in Althochdeutsch.

But the structure itself served a dual purpose.
For while the entrance to the front of the church was open to any who had accepted the Grace of our Lord and the Tax Collectors, the entrance to the rear was of an unholy other sort.

In fact, fully 50% of the building was consecrated as a torture chamber. The walls are graced by iron implements of every kind: thumbscrews, eye gougers, tongue clippers, skull crushers, plus a complete suite of the most contemporary floor models, including skeleton stretching racks and the like.

So in this quaint little town, emblematic of all of Europe at the time, you were going in one door or the other — either to get shorn or to get skinned alive. Along with other persuasions, this may not have been a good time to be a Jew.

# Before it's Too Late

It was another hot summer's day, the cicadas turning into shadows of their former shells, the scorching breath of August turning the asphalt into pudding. I melted through the front door, oozed down the hallway and poured myself onto the bed.

Our cat, Sarah, lay on the floor, an uncharacteristic twinkle in her eye.

That's when I noticed the rat. Gaunt, hungry, odious, likely infested with all manner of parasites — it was hammering its head inside of our loveseat, trapped by the fabric and desperate to escape.

I could only imagine how ugly it must look, and how dangerous it would be once it got out. Although as a Beaches rat, it possibly had enjoyed some civilizing on its long trek into the neighborhood.

I leapt out of bed and grabbed a cane, flipping over the loveseat gingerly. I had read that sometimes they go for your throat.

Sure enough, there was a rat-sized hole ripped into the underside, likely torn asunder in an attempt to elude Sarah. She was quite genteel with those who feed her – but not so much with those she feeds upon.

I saw the unsavory lump wriggle into the back of the couch, and gave it a good, hard whack, but the rat was too fast for me. Startled by this unexpected violence, the cat retreated under the bed. When the rodent scrambled away around the inner coils, I pummeled it remorselessly, but it weaved and dodged at every turn, with the agility of a running back for the New England Patriots.

I was starting to gain respect for my adversary, and I had to take a break to catch my breath, sitting on the edge of the bed for a moment. That's when he stuck his head out of the hole to see if the coast was clear. His red-crested, feathered, pointy-beaked head. Because it wasn't a rat at all; he was a gorgeous, Pileated Woodpecker in all his resplendent glory.

In a flash he made a break for freedom, streaking his way out of the bedroom through the air, down the hall into the living room, out the sliding doors to the terrace and up to the yawning sky above, as if he were a heat-seeking missile.

Fortuitously for us both, he seemed none the worse for wear. And he taught me an essential life lesson about showing good manners to an unexpected guest.

Before it's too late.

# Why are you Here?

Culled from my Facebook interviews in November 2020, asking the question 'Why are you here?'

Cuz.
Perhaps we are all here just to warm the planet.
Water's to blame.
My parents had sex and I popped out.
To properly serve the Art of Storytelling.
I'm here because you asked me to answer your survey.
Where is here?
I am here to create god.
På fb menar du? Eller i din feed?
Wherever you go, there you are.
To redeem the world if ever so slightly.
To get my dopamine levels up when you hit 'Like'.
Choices…choices brought me here.
People, planet, profit, purpose. Celebrating existence.
Leaving a legacy.
So my spirit has a human experience.

Yes.
To be kind and to love God.
To love and experience all facets of love through incarnating.
To normalize critical thinking rather than romantic fantasy.
To uplift the lives of others.
Facebook's algorithm showed your post and so here I am.
To endlessly search for the meaning of life.

Existence predicates quantum entanglements,
If not here, where?
Here is where I am.
I'm a small part of a bigger narrative.
To grow in wisdom and to learn to live better.
The condom broke.
To meet and learn from creative people.
I am here to do the things that need doing.
Better question is "who I'm?"
To teach people about zero-carbon nuclear energy,
our saviour!!!
To impact the world.
God desires the human experience which we all
provide.

I have no idea, but while I am here, I will make the
best of it.
Biology 101, birds and the bees, flowers and the
trees.
I am not here. I am there. Where is there? Playing
chess with a friend.
2 Myers-Briggs models: Sensate: Because I saw your
post. Intuitive: '42'.
Know & love God and contribute to an ever-
advancing civilization.
Teaching po, as a means to move beyond duality.
Life support for my gonads. All else is coincidental,
but I do enjoy it.

To ask this question.

## The Untimely Demise of the Tree House

We lived in the country on 89 acres on the shores of Lake Scugog, where the fish were abundant, the deer bounded through the glades, the glens, the dales and the straths, and the mosquitoes hunted in large packs.

The gardens were designed to bloom in succession, providing an endless array of fragrant visual exquisiosity.

The pond was stocked with Japanese Koi, their resplendent colors moving in counterpoint to the flowers in the breeze. Our daughter, Mackenzie, and I would drive the 4x4 around the water at breakneck speed, and were fortunate enough more than once not to end up in the drink.

In an attempt to offer my daughter a homegrown childhood, I decided to build her a Treehouse. Looking for the right tree was a task unto itself: big enough to bear the weight, with a bifurcated trunk to offer support and enough shade for a hot summer day.

Not really being the handy type, I had no power tools, and even if I had, the nearest electrical outlet was 500 yards away. So I decided to do it the old fashioned way, with hammer and handsaw and square and measuring tape: measuring and sawing, hammering and clawing, then installing the ladder — and the paint was ready to go.

Since Mackenzie was the client, I solicited her input on the color scheme, and once effected, the Treehouse was ready for occupancy.

With great pride, and in anticipation of the many joyous Treehouse-filled times to come, I invited her to ascend the ladder to this personal refuge and home away from home.

I waited with great expectancy as she climbed in. But at once she let out a horrified scream.

'There's a spider in here!!!' she yelled. Once I got her down again, I assured her we could evict the unwelcome intruder and proceed towards happier days.

She looked me seriously in the eye. 'Dad — I'm never, ever going up in that Treehouse again.' My illusions were dashed to pieces.

Luckily, I was able to get her into it one last time, when I put it in a jazz video. So I have the idyllic memory of what could have been, on film at least.

## In Praise of Frogs Everywhere

It's not a frog but it looks like one. Some think it beautiful, the epitome of masculine magnificence despite its underinflated figure. Just look at Michelangelo's David. Ask the Hindu Lingam worshipers. Or consider the attestations of any Frogologist, if you can find one.

But when kissed, this shabby pretender becomes a prince. A pauper that even rises to the stature of an emperor with no clothes in the right hands.
And the jokes afford such gems as 'The water's cold,' said the one; 'And deep,' said the other. Or limericks: 'There was a young man from Kent...' who was so bent out of shape, he ends up going instead of coming.

So it was peculiar to notice on a men's weekend retreat the absence of any 'frog talk', when the purpose was to explore our vulnerabilities honestly. Where were the lengthy discussions? The mirth about girth? And why hadn't it come with any operating instructions?

It's as if any serious talk about questions of dimension when not at attention were heresy, breaking millennia of convention and good taste. I mean, a fleeting glance in the locker room was allowed if it was committed in error. But that was about the extent of it.

So when the group went skinny dipping in a show of false bravado, the contortions required to avoid any appearance of curiosity were enough to call for the services of a chiropractor.

But after a bit of splashing about in the near-freezing water, there we were, eight of us in a circle, standing in the lake in a semi-squat, discussing our inner fears and our aspirations for emancipation from them, without addressing the most obvious and unavoidable issue, one clearly staring us squarely in the face: Whose is longer and how long is it really anyway?

Inevitably the conversation flagged, the tension was building, our legs were getting tired, and there seemed to be no way to escape the trap the Unconscious had set. So I made a suggestion. 'Why don't we all get this over with and just stand up?'

The horror was evident in everybody's face, but slowly we all began to rise in the water. And sure enough, there wasn't a single example of Homo Erectus in the bunch. You would have needed calipers to tell any difference at all, and even they would have fallen within the margin of error.

Afterwards, we all breathed a sigh of relief, and things seemed to be lighter for the rest of the workshop. Reduced to approximately 2 ounces apiece, in fact, but I'm only guessing of course. I hadn't been looking that closely.

## Isaac: Lord of the Seal Hunt

Isaac was a prolific hunter – canny, brave and with a 'seal-sense' that guided him unerringly to his quarry. He could haul in the bounty like he was shopping for canned sardines. At least, to hear him tell it.

I had asked him to take us seal hunting for months, but something always came up that got in the way.
His girlfriend quietly told us he had a reputation among The People for having bad luck, but they were just being polite.

His eyesight was bad they said and he couldn't shoot straight even if it hadn't been.

Whenever he picked up a rifle everybody high-tailed it for the hills. Luckily he was also hard of hearing, so he was spared the terrorized screams of the faint of heart and the guffaws of those who knew better.

Because Isaac couldn't even hit somebody by mistake.
Finally the evasion had become so glaring that one day he made the Grand Announcement. We were all going on a seal hunt.

The boat was floated, the fuel was checked, the motor fired up. The guns were loaded and the horizon was scanned with furrowed brow.

Then came what I understood to be a finger test of the wind, a sniffing of the air for spoor, a careful survey of the wave patterns, analysis of the disposition of ice floes and some kind of ritualistic vigorous scratching of the head, gnashing of the teeth and pulling of facial hair that went on interminably.

Suddenly he sat down and turned off the motor, without having left the dock. 'No seal today,' he pronounced. Apparently the seal ran on a tight schedule and we had missed the boat. It really didn't ring true, though. so we all clamored for the hunt. He began to sweat and his hands started shaking, but his self-induced reputation was at stake. So off we went.

After an hour or so with Isaac guiding our hunting party we had come up with nothing. A few times I thought I saw a seal jumping in the distance, but Isaac wisely advised us that it was nothing but a trick of the eyes. Probably his, we guessed.

Then one launched out of the water just 100 yards away. Isaac pretended not to see the creature, 'to avoid spooking it', he said. But once we got closer (and he could see it) the need for swift action was inescapable, and Isaac grabbed his rifle and fired in one rapid movement, without even taking the time to aim.

His girlfriend ducked, so unfortunately she couldn't independently verify Isaac's account.

But apparently Isaac shot him right between the eyes, so he exclaimed. Sadly, when we went to investigate, it was nowhere to be seen, without even a drop of blood left as evidence of the kill. Isaac explained that it had sunk immediately, due to the power of his shot.

"Home now," he commanded.

After all, he got what he came for. He now had a whale of a tale to recount to everybody at fire that night, and he was anticipating the joyous belly laughs that typically accompanied such prowess on one of his hunts.

What he could hear of them.

# Beau Talks

Certainly big pharmaceutical companies have helped
to transform the healthcare landscape for the better
with a broad array of medicines that ameliorate a
range of afflictions — not the least of which are the
breakthroughs in vaccine development for COVID-
19.

But once in a very short while, the industry careens
off a moral cliff and its marketing communications
firms hit a brick wall on the way down.

Such was the case with a now widely available drug
whose name I will not mention here. And that is part
of the story.

Government regulations stipulate that the name of a
prescription drug product cannot be mentioned in the
same advertisement that explains what it is for and
why you should convince your doctor to prescribe it.
Together with expenses-paid 'information sessions'
in Hawaii for physicians, consumer freebees and
other persuasion tools, the pressure to make the right
choice would be overwhelming.

So the message-makers are reduced to platitudes
such as 'Talk to your doctor for effective solutions'
and the like.

But the launch of the new drug was to be different.
The mission was to find a way to get around the legal

obstacles and present an unfettered message free of the encumbrance.

When I sat in the boardroom of the Ad Agency that conceived the idea, I was astounded.

Since the product purported to make the lines and wrinkles in one's face disappear instantaneously, the proposal was to create a healthcare expert named Beau. And this was no run-of-the-mill healthcare expert.

He was a Shar-Pei dog, renowned for their fissure-faced, wrinkled skin.

He would give wholesome, skin-smoothing advice in TV spots, in print ads and on the Internet. The segments and articles would be entitled 'Beau Talks'!

So the storyboards were drawn up, the ads created and the Agency presented to the Client.

Oddly, after considerable analysis, the idea was nixed in favor of a campaign message that was also compelling. The breakthrough idea was simply to 'Talk to your doctor for effective solutions.'

There! I said 'Beau Talks', and I never even mentioned the name of the product. Honest...

## On the Art of PFFFlatury

'Afflatus' is derivative of the Latin 'afflatus', past
participle of afflare, "to blow at or breathe on," from
ad-, "at" + flare, "to puff, to blow."
Other words with the same root include:
deflate (de-, "out of" + flare);
inflate (in-, "into" + flare);
soufflé, the "puffed up" dish (from French souffler,
"to puff," from Latin sufflare,
"to blow from below," hence "to blow up, to puff
up," from sub-, "below" + flare)…
…and above all:
flatulent.
The latter may be related to the hot air emitted by
politicians and the like, especially during campaign
season.

## Stab City

A town in Ireland named Limerick
Is renowned the world o'er for its word tricks
But their manners aren't witty
It's oft called Stab City
'Cause their greetings are made using ice-picks.

# My Secret Problem

I knew I had a problem. It was always obvious I was different. It started when I was lying in bed one night and I noticed I had a lump in my throat. I thought it was a tumor, but the doctor said it was my Adam's Apple.

Fine for him, but he didn't notice it was on crooked, embarrassingly off center. I was sure everybody was talking about it. I heard them whispering as I went by and I think they may have been talking about me.

Worse than that, my lips were too big. And they were too red. It looked like I had lipstick on, but I swear I never did. That wouldn't have been so bad. But I had to keep them closed to hide my teeth.

I sucked my thumb for years, and I could tell I was getting buck teeth. It was only a matter of time until I looked like Fred Palmer down the street. His were so bad, nobody would let him play baseball. What's worse, he didn't even know why. And the more I thought about it, the worse they got.

I knew that sooner or later, somebody at the playground was going to scream 'He's got Buck Teeth!, and my life would be over before I had the chance to feel up a girl at some point in the future.

My hair parted on the wrong side. It was just like Hitler's, my dad said. I didn't know who he was, but

I sure didn't want to be like him. We couldn't make it part the other way no matter how hard we tried.

I used both my hands to write with, one then the other, but at school my teachers told me I was only supposed to use the right one. I had to write, 'I will only use my right hand,' over and over again on the chalkboard.

I never liked playing sports. I thought I might be cross-eyed. Sometimes my nose would bleed for no reason.

My father gave me a watch inscribed with my name, and I was so proud of it, I walked around throwing it up in the air and catching it. Until I missed and it smashed in pieces on the sidewalk.

The dog next door liked me, though.
Once I dropped a nickel down my throat by mistake and for days I waited for it to come out. But I think it's still in there somewhere.

Sometimes I used to stare in the mirror for hours, looking deep into my own eyes and wondering who I really was. My mom would laugh and tell me not to be so silly. I was Ross she said. She said I think too much. But I didn't really believe her.

And no matter how much I tried to ignore it, I started to think my teachers were stupid and that my parents didn't know anything at all.

That's when my problems really began.

## The Roughneck

We are pulling a mile of metal pipe out of the oil well.

I'm operating the tongs, a hydraulic machine that grasps the pipe as it is pulled out, while spinning it out of the collar of the one below.

Once released, the thirty-foot stand is yanked back and over my head  to join its brothers, so we can change the diamond drill bit, worn by biting though solid rock.

On the way through the air, its saline contents are disgorged, soaking me from head to toe, and freezing on contact. This tortuous ritual is to be repeated nearly two hundred times over the course of a 12-hour shift, until three inches of ice covers my skidoo suit and I can barely move my arms.

The only thing that keeps me going is imagining I am twisting the Driller's head off with every turn.

After a time, I notice the tongs have a different pitch in their whine, depending on how fast I turn them.

Soon, I am able to play songs on them and become quite proficient, even composing some of my own melodies.

Then, that familiar spattering, as our Derrick man urinates on us from forty feet up the rig. Seniority gives him the right and it's not much worse than everything else.

You have to be careful up there. The well can blow in, covering anything in sight with slimy, cold, crude oil. Plugging it with a Stabbing Valve while your face is covered in gushing petroleum, can be almost impossible.

If it catches on fire, which it is inclined to do, you'd better get out of the way in a hurry.

You also have to be careful not to catch a finger as the pipe flies up and you have to yank it back, or you'll join it on its way.

And if the rig starts to fall over, a hundred feet of metal writhing like a snake, you've got about ten seconds to jump on the escape line and wheel down to safety ahead of it.

But up there, sometimes, I would gaze in the distance as the feather-brush jackpines tickled the fancy of Heaven.

And I felt strangely at home.

## The Last Fish

There are moments in life when there is a planetary alignment and you know almost everything is going to go your way.

It's a good time to buy lottery tickets. It's a good time to go on a heavy date. It's *not* a good time to go salmon fishing.

I'd been at it for two hours. With Ashbridges Bay all to myself early in the morning, I was certain I was all but guaranteed to haul in the grand-daddy of them all.

I tried a Mepps Spinner No. 5. No luck. Then a Silver Shadow. Nope! I pulled out a Johnston Weedless Spoon. Obviously the salmon had never heard of it.

In rapid succession came a Rapala Husky Jerk. A Magnum Musky Killer, a Comet Mino. And every combination of spinners, jigs and hooks imaginable.

Even the worms had broken out and were wriggling away into the bushes to get away from me.

Just as the planets achieved a perfect alignment and a hush descended upon the land, I heard heavy footsteps coming through the bushes.

A fisherman stepped out and sniffed the air, creel over his shoulder, an Eddie Bauer vented Boonie Hat perfectly draped on his head, with chest waders and two Fenwick fly rods.

The sun flashed across his Balmain sunglasses as he quietly hopped out into the water, landing on a rock.

In one graceful move, he flicked his fly rod, allowing the Tufted Mantis to settle.

In a moment it was snapped up and he pulled out the most beautiful fish, 30 inches long, with a glorious greenish hue. Just as adroitly, my arch-enemy pivoted ever-so-gracefully and leapt to shore, vanishing into the greenery.

Slowly I packed up my gear and trudged home. With thoughts of the finest fish I never caught, and the idle thought that I might take up a less stressful hobby.

Say, polo for instance.

## Mom's New Hat

There comes a time when each of us is cast out of The Garden without so much as a 'by your leave.'

My mother had had another baby and suffered post-partum depression. When I was six, it was called a nervous breakdown.

My father looked down on me and said 'Ross, your mother is in the hospital and she needs your support. You're going to have to start helping out around here more.' He did have five other kids and a job, of course.

Although I didn't know what that really meant, I agreed. It later became apparent that it included learning to dress properly, tie my shoes, stop sucking my thumb, do some dishes, wash the kitchen floor, do my homework and stop running around the house and making noise so much.

Once, she sent me a note:
*'Dear Fossy:* (for such was my pet name)
*I am sick, but I'll be home soon. Please be good and help your father. I'll always love you!*
*Mummy'*

When she came home, things were never the same. She had had shock treatments, several dozen of them, and was highly medicated.

I had waited weeks for her to arrive, but when she did, she didn't seem to see me at all, even when she was looking right at me.

They told me she was depressed, but I thought she was just sad. I kept trying to think of a way to make her happy again, but I couldn't.

Then everything became wrong with me and I didn't know what to do about it. I forgot how to tie my shoes. My clothes weren't on right. My face was always dirty and so were my fingernails. My schoolwork was no good. There were schoolyard gangs and I had to fight them.

And all the while, I waited for her to come back to life, but she didn't.

Then one day I saw it. A quaint little ladies' hat store on Bloor Street, somewhere I wasn't allowed to go. 'It's far too dangerous!' But in the window was a beautiful lady's hat on a stand and I knew it would bring the sparkle back to her eyes.

Every day I would stop by the window on my way to school to make certain the hat was still there, and it was. One day I screwed up the nerve to go in and ask how much it cost. $5.95 the lady told me.

I only had two bits. So that seemed impossible. But I was making a little money turning on the stove for the old folks down the street during Shabbat, and somebody else paid me to take out their garbage, so there was hope.

But one day, my heart fell out. It was gone. Somebody had bought it.

When I got home, she was angry. 'Where have you been??? I hope you weren't on Bloor Street again!'
I knew my life would never be the same after that.

The lady I loved was gone.

## The Center of the World

You haven't been anywhere if you haven't been to the Center of the World.

It's not New York and it's not Los Angeles, Beijing, Tokyo, Moscow, Buenos Aires, New Delhi, Berlin, Riyadh or Tel Aviv.

But when I was there, I got the feeling that this is where world policy is decided. I figured the Bilderberg Group meets here. The Masons probably perform secret rituals right out in the open.

This is likely where the Scientologists conspire, where the Russian Federal Security Service plans world domination, where CIA agents pretend they work at the FBI and where the Pope and Dalai Lama get together incognito to shoot the breeze after changing their costumes.

And I think the reason it's such a secret is that nobody can remember what they talked about when they were there. The mind control technology is that good.

Where is this secret gathering place hiding in plain sight? If I told you I'd have to have your brain dry-cleaned and your ears washed out with soap.

Luckily that won't be necessary.

For those with their noses to the ground, here's a clue as to its whereabouts:

Distance to:

| | |
|---|---|
| Beijing | 8,280 km. |
| Berlin | 1,705 km. |
| Buenos Aires | 10,985 km. |
| New York City | 5,112 km. |
| Los Angeles | 8,300 km. |
| Moscow | 2,820 km. |
| New Delhi | 7,080 km. |
| Riyadh | 6,989 km. |
| Tel Aviv | 4,023 km. |
| Tokyo | 9,588 km. |

If they let you in after you get to the fifth floor, you can see the world without leaving your bar stool.

And you'll be on top of the world before you know it. Sláinte!

## Styrofoam Garbage Day

I wrote a commercial where a Jeep Grand Cherokee blows through a snowbank, atomizing it, as a snowman looks on. His head twists around in circles from the force of the impact.

The client bought it and we were on our way. Except that it was during a heat wave in the middle of summer, so there was no snow to be had.

With my genius FX guy, Tom, and looking forward to endless hours in the animation studio painting in ambient snow, we had the perfect shot. Once only, my DP and I agreed, since we couldn't rebuild the Styrofoam 'snowbank' once it had been blown apart.

All went as planned, other than the 2,000 shards of Styrofoam strewn all over the location. And for some inexplicable reason, my props guy had a sudden appointment somewhere else.

He did agree to load my pickup, but I had to talk him into tying it off. 'It's all secure,' he smiled.

After he left, I had a look and saw that every crevice of the bed had been stuffed into submission, with a mountain of Styrofoam sometimes reaching seven feet high. All 'secured' by the thinnest ball of string you can get.

And I had thirty miles of highway driving on what was now a dark and windy night.

Gritting my teeth, I made it fifteen miles before the first piece of string broke. Then another.

I had to get off the highway and onto a service road, but what you gain in peace of mind, you lose in velocity.

Finally I crawled into the garbage depot in the city and parked the truck and its contents until the next day, when they would open.

In the morning, I drove onto the weigh scale. The operator looked up from his Monster Truck magazine long enough to say, 'We don't accept Styrofoam here. You have to take it to Depot #16. It's about five miles across town.'

At a complete loss, I pulled outside the depot and shut off the engine. So close, yet so far.

Then, Heaven interceded with a giant gust of wind, breaking the remaining binding and blowing all the Styrofoam up against the Depot fence.

The operator looked up from his magazine for a moment and then went back to the job he had at hand.

# Canadian Long Weekend

The annual event was legendary. Three days of the best pickerel fishing in the bush at Fisherman's Bluff, with a dozen hardy buddies who had been at it for a dozen years without fail or wives. I was honored to be invited.

It took three hours to get there, wending my way through a dirt trail, almost hanging up on the rocks and bogging down in the muskeg. Finally, I pulled up to the camp, and the celebrations were already underway.

The fire was crackling, the alcohol flowed freely, the porn movies were playing and the cards were on the table. It was all part of a ritual leading to the Great Fishing Expedition.

Not one to spoil the fun, I knocked back some Screech, pulled up a chair and lit a smoke. Now I do enjoy a civilized round of Bridge or two, punctuated by some intelligent discourse and an insightful joke or two.

But guessing what the perfect female company is to enjoy a good beer wasn't one of them. Something like three feet high with lipstick and a perfectly flat head. It reminded me of my days as a Derrickman on the oil rigs.

I wasn't much better at Poker, especially since they kept switching games every hand.

Acey-Duecy, Flip the Jack, Razz, Follow the Queen, Billabong, Blow the Load — the only explanation of the rules was the occasional grunt and a coughing fit once the gange came out.

47

Once or twice as my stake was plummeting towards zero, I blurted out something conversational like 'When are we going fishing?' or some such nonsense.

At times like these, everybody would stop dead and stare at me quizzically for a moment, then go back to the carnage.

I ran out of money rapidly and that's when the farting started. It quickly became a competition; then it morphed into 12-part harmony punctuated by belching and gales of laughter.

All this joy riven by orgiastic cries of the carnal variety emanating from the video tape.

To escape the torture, I bolted, grabbing my fishing rod and plunging into the darkness towards the dock. Collapsing in a heap to catch my breath, I started casting into the water — whipping it out of anguish, really — to no avail.

After hours of slapping the waves and myself into submission, the awful truth dawned on me. There are no fish at Fisherman's Bluff. It was given that name to catch fishermen and turn them into poker players who get filleted for every penny they've got.

When I got back to the cabin, I was met by air so thick you could open a Limburger cheese shop, accompanied by a cacophony of snoring in three octaves.

Like a cat burglar, I grabbed my pack and stole away into the night, only daring to draw a full breath of air once I hit the highway. It must have been the shortest long weekend in history.

# Prime Minister Justin Trudeau – Up Close and Personal

I conducted this interview for Waterfront Magazine after the Prime Minister's first election victory, in an effort to explore his more personal side.

Ross Ulysses Munroe: Can you tell us about a defining personal experience that helped to drive your commitment to preserving the Environment?

*My family's relationship with the outdoors – with Canada's natural beauty – has been a lifelong one for me. My dad taught us Trudeau boys how to paddle a canoe almost as soon as we could walk. And like many Canadians, I've spent many summer nights out under the stars, beside a campfire, getting eaten alive by mosquitoes and black flies. My dad was never a fan of bug spray. I've always believed that when it comes to our environment, we Canadians get it. We appreciate its beauty, understand its dangers, and know its value.*

Ross Ulysses Munroe: Please tell us about personal experiences earlier in your life that contributed to your very proactive stance on helping refugees immigrate to Canada.

*I was aware very early on that the country we know and love was built by those who fled oppression, famine, and war – those who left everything behind to start anew in a strange and faraway land. My father was a champion of multiculturalism. He taught me that dialogue, conviction, and compassion constitute the only real path toward peace and understanding. Above all, he taught me that what unites us is far greater than what divides us.*

*As Canadians, we take great pride in our history of opening our arms and our borders to those in need, no matter one's faith, culture, or where they're from. We define ourselves through our compassion, and know we have a responsibility to continue opening our doors to our most vulnerable neighbours around the world.*

*It was an honour to personally greet several Syrian refugee families earlier this year when they landed in Canada. Meeting them one by one, and seeing the delight in their eyes, only reinforced my beliefs.*

Ross Ulysses Munroe: One might consider the results of the last election as the repudiation of individual selfish goals, in favour of a commitment to the common good of Canadian society and our support of people around the world. To what degree do you agree with this, and could you comment?

*I think the campaign we ran was based on putting fear aside and choosing instead to have confidence in Canada, Canadians, and the fundamental values that have come to define this country. We embraced hard work – not cynicism. We beat out negative, divisive politics with a positive, hopeful vision to bring Canadians together.*

*Across the country, at every campaign stop, I told Canadians, "In Canada, better is always possible." I think that this optimism, along with our pledge to accept 25,000 Syrian refugees, and our promise to make government more open and transparent resonated not only with Canadians – but with people around the world.*

Ross Ulysses Munroe: To what degree is your political career informed by the example and insight afforded to you by your father?

*When I think about my father's work-life balance, I think of it in terms of how he brought us with him on so many world trips – that having us along with him kept him balanced and made him a better leader.*

*Before I became Prime Minister, when I used to drive back to Montréal, after three days in Ottawa, I would look back and ask myself, "Okay, did the work I do in Ottawa contribute to a world that is better enough to compensate for the fact that I wasn't there to put my kids to bed for three nights in a row? Having this touchstone – linking this important job to real life and real people and a real impact on a human level – is something that my father modeled for me.*

Ross Ulysses Munroe: I have a theory that Canada had an identity crisis because it has no national ego in the way many countries do (nationalism, etc.). And that now that we have grown up to be such a robustly multicultural society, we are reflecting the characteristics of the ideal global citizenry - tolerant, compassionate, egalitarian. What is your feeling about this?

*We are a nation of millions of immigrants and refugees, of hundreds of cultures, languages, and religions, who are bound by one, unshakable belief: we are stronger not in spite of our differences, but precisely because of them.*

*Peace, freedom, respect, compassion, inclusivity, and diversity – these are our cherished Canadian values.*

*As Canada moves toward a greater leadership role in the world, I am confident that these values will remain synonymous with the maple leaf, 'Canada' and 'Canadian.'*

## Arresting Myself

Just before I left to hitch-hike down East, my friend Esther gave me a denim strap with a heart on it, to wrap around my thigh.

After a day or two and a steady stream of chatty truckers, I got a ride with a rugged looking country boy about 40.

After a bit of back and forth about Hank Snow and truck rallies, he got right to the point.

'Look, you *are* into it, aren't you?' 'Into what?' I replied.

'Don't play games with me, you wouldn't be hitch-hiking out here if you weren't looking,' he said casually. Then he did a double take, reevaluating. 'Sooner or later you're going to have to try it. What do you want?'

'I want you to let me off at the next truck stop.'

A few minutes later, he pulled up to one, muttering under his breath and I got out.

It was getting late, but I had to keep going.

The next driver, a corpulent, greedy sort of fellow with a wandering eye and puffy lips, launched right into it. 'My last lover had a wang so big, it took two hands to get a hold of it and there was plenty left then too!'

Luckily I arrived at my destination, a deserted cornfield in the middle of nowhere. I took comfort in the fact that I had packed a 6" knife, and he was kind enough to let me out once he got the idea.

Near midnight, it was raining as my next driver pulled over. 'Where you heading tonight?' he inquired, looking me over. By now, I was used to it.

'Beaverbrooke,' I said.

Well, why do you have that garter belt on your leg anyway? Who do you know in Beaverbrooke — and where are you staying???'

'The Police Station. Can you drop me there?'

Twenty minutes later I was lying in an old stone cell, courtesy of the local constabulary.

On the wall, someone had etched 'I'm wanted for grand theft in Prince Rupert. They're after me for assault in Buffalo Narrows, and here I am sleeping under their noses in Beaverbrooke.'

I slept well. And the next day, I removed Esther's traveling gift for the rest of the trip.

# Reindeer Racing in Lapland

You've got to watch the vodka up there. My pal, Olaf Chistiansson, went into a three-day retreat in the sauna; he slipped and sat on the hot rocks nudie-bums and couldn't peel himself off. After a week in the Helsinki hospital, he still couldn't sit down.

In the bar, the flavored vodka never stopped flowing. Men would stand stoically for hours, only to fall like bowling pins almost in unison. A couple would come dancing full tilt across the floor and crash headlong into the sound system, collapsing without missing a beat.

My client at Finnish National Airlines asked me to compose a headline about what makes this ancient country so unique. My answer was: 'It's just like Canada, only farther.'

He took us out to his family's sauna in the bush. It had been handed down for 250 years and it was charred from all the burning wood over that time. Once we were ushered through the door starkers, we were covered head to foot with ice water.

Then there was the ice hotel. They have a lot of the stuff in Lapland, so they're always looking for something to do with it. It's a bad real estate investment though.
But the highlight was the reindeer racing, where we roared around the ice track pulled by these grand ungulates, led by Santa Claus himself.

Then he was on his way. He had 40 ounces of Finlandia he hadn't lit into yet. And a reputation to uphold.

## Earl's War

He was in his eighties when I met him, and we became friends.

His wife had passed years before and his kids had grown up and moved away. So he was left alone with his thoughts, mostly about The Great War.

He served as a suicide gunner, his machine gun rattling off bullets so his buddies could retreat, until the barrel began to melt. They couldn't see him through the smoke, and he would slaughter hundreds of the 'Boche' charging after his comrades.

Of course, sooner or later he was also expected to die for the Cause. Which he did.

When the medics found him, he had been shot twice, bayoneted once and poisoned by mustard gas. During his demise, his body had swelled to twice its usual size.

A letter of condolence was sent to his parents describing how he died a hero in the service of his country and that his remains would remain in France.
Imagine their surprise when he disembarked in Halifax, clambering off the boat and making his way home to Hamilton.

Earl got married after that and had children, then grandkids and more. But he never really left his foxhole, where he stared into the faces of the young boys he had killed, and wondered aloud 'What for?'

# Working at Home

Managing yourself is one of the most difficult challenges you'll ever encounter. Rather than face this daunting task, people will do almost anything else, including:

blaming it on the client - because he/she is too small-minded

blaming it on the boss - because he/she doesn't appreciate your genius

blaming it on the co-workers - because they are jealous

blaming it on the parents - because they're easy marks

The problem with these approaches is that they are self-defeating. Although they relieve you of responsibility for your life, they also sabotage your life because the only person who will be able to overcome all these challenges is you.

And if you give your power to other people in your own mind, you are selling the only asset you have complete control over. Your own choice.

If, on the other hand, you are committed to doing the best work, something highly unusual will occur.

You will produce remarkable work you can be proud of, that sets you apart from anybody else and serves the interests of all concerned. Because it is your own integrity and authenticity that are shining through all of it.

And why would you pretend to be somebody else?

Something that will occur with you doesn't occur as readily with people in other lines of work. If you're a steelworker, an occupational hazard is that you may fall into a vat of molten metal and die.

If you're sitting at home alone drilling down into your subconscious mind to uncover ideas nobody else has thought of, you may end up facing some things in there that most people don't really think about that much:

Uncomfortable memories.

Scenes from your childhood.

Repressed feelings suddenly laid bare.

Philosophical questions about the nature of existence.

Erratic thinking.

Inexplicable urges from the limbic brain.

Hypochondria.

Etc.

Don't be surprised. You are digging into the collective unconscious, and the entire universe is there waiting for you. But it isn't there to overwhelm or threaten you. It is there as a resource you can mine forever - never having to repeat yourself unless you want to, always having that mountain of consciousness and ideas to draw upon.

Always remember - your infinite imagination is there to serve you and your purpose. It was never meant to be taken too seriously.

# Sonny & Brownie Go On Another Bender

It wasn't their fault, but Sonny was blind and Brownie couldn't walk.

Brownie could pick his way around a six-string better than a tightrope-walking ballerina with a half a dozen fingers. Sonny could bend the notes on his harp until they wailed like a banshee in heat. And their 35-year-long partnership helped to define Folk/Blues, with their Piedmont style that incorporated folk and ragtime overtones into the Blues.

In this genre, nobody was more active in the studio, on stage and on tour than Sonny Terry and Brownie McGhee.

I saw them later in their careers, where I got a personal take of their love for foot-stomping 'wine, wine, wine' by the jug on stage, and later, in the back room, between sets.
When I got back there, they were guzzling the stuff to beat the band. But of course, they were the band, so that was their right. I may have joined them in a little too much of it…

Meanwhile, their main squeeze was back there, pouring liberally, a corpulent white belle in her late fifties. And after all these decades, the duo was competing for her attentions with all the fervour they could manage.

Sonny did this, he bragged. Brownie did that. The woman was enraptured, having practiced the part for years.  I never could tell which one she was conferring her favours on. But it was time for more 'wine, wine, wine', and we all stumbled back to the audience to prove the point. Brownie stumbled a lot more than the rest of us, of course, and to no one's surprise, Sonny bumped his head on the microphone, almost knocking the PA system over.

# Windowpane

I felt as though I was in a John le Carré novel.

If anybody was in dire need of a little LSD to spice up life and open the mind, it had to be the people in the Province of Newfoundland & Labrador.

I was only 18, but I was an entrepreneur in the making.

I had one of those belts with double belt prongs, and I used an Exacto knife to cut it open, creating a small pocket impervious to prying eyes.

Then I slid 200 hits of windowpane acid in the slot, sewing it up tight again. With a purchase price of a buck apiece and a sale price three times that, I was sure I'd net a tidy sum — paying for my summer adventure, at least.

I became very popular once I crossed the New Brunswick border. Somehow the locals had heard about me and showed up at the hostel in Saint John for a score. I sold ten in one night.

In Truro, I unloaded another dozen, and more in North Sydney, waiting for the ferry. There was a government workers strike on there, so the liquor store and the police were out. As a consequence, the windows were all broken, and both the whiskey and the thrill had evaporated. I had a ready market and made the most of it.

A storm blew in during the ferry ride to The Rock, and I left the better part of myself over the side.

Once on the island, I had a long ride to St. John's from Argentia, spending a night in the bush terrified I was going to be eaten by a bear.

Finally I got to the hostel and found a private place to cut open my belt and survey my wares. Just as a gust of North Atlantic wind blew them all over the floor.

Now, windowpane acid is completely transparent and the items are only about one eighth of an inch square. Against an old wood floor, there isn't much to see.

So after glumly touring the town for a few days, I began the 1500-mile trek back home, where I started looking for another line of work.

## A Bat out of Hell

I had a pet bat once, I caught him one night. I put him in a bamboo birdcage. He wasn't of the bloodsucking variety, thankfully.

He stayed for a day or two while he got his rest & fill. Then he squeezed through the bars. I didn't know it, of course, but they're like mice, mostly cartilage, and can compress to a fraction of their operating size.

He thought he was making a clean getaway, I guess. But I had a cat at the time, who was going bat-shit crazy himself. The lucky bat outmaneuvered him like the one out of hell for a couple of days.

Sadly, one evening they became too well acquainted and had dinner together. Nothing remained but a big Cheshire smile, licking its chops smugly.

# 100 Things I Love

Massenet's Thais Meditation.
Sake Sashimi.
Sing, Sing, Sing by Benny Goodman.
Making whoopee with my wife.
Dreamwork.
Editing Waterfront magazine unless I'm taking a
sabbatical.

Planting Morning Glories.
Bees & cicadas.
Dancing up a storm with Arielle, Mackenzie &
Dallas.

Luminous ice floes gathering in the morning in
Frobisher Bay.
Zardoz.
Playing All Along The Watchtower on guitar.
Doing the Tai Chi on the pier down the street.
Directing story-driven jazz videos.
Kool klothes.
Rumblefish.
Camping beside the Yukon River.
Virginia's Lamb & Linguini Pasta.

My faux fur rabbit skin winter hat.
Flying to Europe.
Fishing in the Baltic Sea.
A good Pinot Grigio.
Repartee with a great friend.
Brazil by Terry Gilliam.

The sound of all the farm animals waking each other
up to greet the day, rolling across the hills in Munster
Ireland.

Tides.
The Battle of Thermopylae.
Chess.
Writing a short story about ants.
Singing Auld Lang Syne.
Friedensreich Regentag Dunkelbunt Hundertwasser.
Montserrat before the volcano blew its top.

Christmas decorations.
Tal Wilkenfeld's bass solo on 'Cause We've Ended
As Lovers.

Tartufo.
The Portable Jung.
Elephant funeral processions.
Doing chakra energy work.
No Trump Bridge.
Ran by Akira Kurosawa
Lord of the Rings.
Gorgonzola cheese.
Reindeer racing in Lapland.

The Washington Post.
Towering clouds.
Amazing Grace on Bagpipes.
Flags of the world.
Ancient military tactics.
Marc Chagall.
Nessun Dorma by Pavarotti.

Zen Flesh, Zen Bones.
Parma Prosciutto.
Ly O Lay Ale Loya.
Cats & dogs if not raining.
Active imagination.

McArthur's Universal Corrective Map of the World.
Mount Fuji.
One armed bandits in Macau.
Italian sculptor Francesco Queirolo
Pan flutists.

Cream cheese with capers, lemon & lox.
Modern medicine
An iron fist in a velvet glove.
Listening to languages I don't understand.
The Messiah by Roy Buchanan.
The tinkling of cowbells drifting through the Swiss
Alps.

Practical philosophy.
My birth family.
Santa Monica.

The Index in Harper's Magazine.
Didgeridoo music.
Alternative therapy.
Stick-figure storyboarding.
Sundogs.
Women.

Django Reinhardt & Stephane Grappelli.

Wolves howling.
Casting for a production.
Sunshine.
Buying fresh fruit.
Haiku.

Playing Foggy Mountain Breakdown on the banjo.
Fly fishing.
Doing the Two Dagger knife set (until I forgot it).
Hot tubbing with a glass of wine.

Stimulating metaphysical conversations with
Virginia.

Hakomi body-centered psychotherapy.
Speeding around corners in a stick shift.
Weight training.
Songbirds as the sun rises.
Duckbilled platypuses.
Riding a Motorcycle.
Archery.

Sleeping.
The call of a loon across the lake.
Castles carved into mountainsides in Germany.
Austin Healeys.
Calculus.
Exoskeletons.
The Om.

# Repositioning Beano

The reality of passing gas is bad enough, but it is made much less offensive than its Saxon cousins by using the Latinesque term 'flatulence.' At least that takes the wind out of its sails, leaving only the banal reality of its immutable existence hanging in the air, especially after a heaping helping of 'the musical fruit.'

The problem for the makers of Beano was their product didn't pass the smell test, when it came to side-stepping the crass nature of the problem it was intended to alleviate. 'Beano – for flatulence' just didn't have a ring to it or even anything remotely appealing about it. But that's why we have marketing companies. The idea was to rename the affliction to make it more scientific-sounding, and build market share by making it socially acceptable. Like many things it's a sickness and anybody can get it.

So a new term was invented. Complex Carbohydrate Intolerance or a convenient CCI for short. Do you have CCI? Millions of spinach and broccoli eating consumers do. With the nasty consequences just waiting to embarrass you in public or even with a loved one.

Medical studies were commissioned. Communications programs were developed. But in the focus groups, despite the prevalence of lactose intolerance, peanut allergies and the like, 'that word' would always come up.

Sooner or later, somebody would look around the room at all the guilty faces and sheepishly say 'Look, it's really just Farting'. Then everybody would break out laughing. And that was the end of that.

The next challenge? Curing unpalatable stomach noises. Concept? Run a contest to give them a scientific name…

## Pat Paulson Walks on Water

I always loved Pat Paulson on the Smothers Brothers Comedy Hour with his dour demeanour, his rugged bad looks and his acerbic wit. A few of his observations:

'All the problems we face in the United States today can be traced to an unenlightened immigration policy on the part of the American Indian.'

'Should we continue to spend billions to subsidize foreign military dictatorships? Or should we concentrate on taking better care of the one we have right here at home?'

'Let's face it — we need guns. You never can tell: when you're walking down the street, you might spot a moose. And how about suicide? Can you imagine trying to beat yourself to death with a stick?'

'We of the Smothers Brothers Comedy Hour have had our share of censorship problems. However, we are not against censorship because we realize there is always the danger of something being said.'

'Assuming either the Left Wing or the Right Wing gained control of the country, it would probably fly around in circles.'

'We have nothing to fear but fear itself. And the boogey man.'

So when he announced he was running for President, I knew his policies were right up my alley. And while his campaign stop in Seattle occurred in Victoria by mistake, as a BC native I considered it to be a case of Divine Intervention.

He was slated to make a special appearance by the Georgia Strait, demonstrating his divinity by actually walking on water, a promise not much farther fetched than those of his Establishment opponents.

On the day, the crowds were everywhere, including scuba divers, seagulls, local celebrities, politicians and the Press. Everybody waited for Candidate Paulson to arrive, and sure enough his limousine rolled into view and stopped in front of the pier.

The oompah-pah band his team had hired began playing Hail to the Chief, as he paused for photos and waved to the crowd. Then he turned and marched with great purpose out along the pier, taking his first step onto the water.

Nobody could really have predicted the gravity of the situation that unfolded next. For some reason he plunged down and right out of sight.

At first, nothing could be seen. Then a flailing arm broke the surface and the scuba divers made a beeline for the man. After he struggled back to shore, he coughed and sputtered and huffed and puffed.

His hair was a terrible mess.

Once he regained his poise, the Press asked him what went wrong. 'Deep down, I happen to be very shallow,' he said.

You couldn't blame the man for breaking his campaign promise, though. As his website said recently: 'Pat ran his campaign using outright lies, double talk and unfounded attacks on his challengers. Who thought that this style would be the method of campaigns in the future?'

# Deer Run

I cared for her. I did.

But in a dream, when I heard that a nuclear weapon had exploded in my office with her name on it, it was unsettling to say the least. As the fallout began and the landscape was changed forever, the dream shifted to a lush woodland.

I had become a stag and she was a doe, both of us racing in leaps and bounds to join the herd as it receded over the hills, the sun and the future beckoning in the distance. We were late.

But we were lagging behind the rest, and as the mass of bodies picked up speed, she began to stumble, ultimately tripping on a fallen tree trunk. I stopped and tried to help her regain her footing.

She looked up at me plaintively. Then her bowels fell out. She could go no further. I leaned down and she softly told me she would be alright. I kissed her. Then I turned towards my receding companions.

There was a lot of ground to cover.

My legs retracted into my body and my hide was transformed into burnished titanium. I began to fly. The sun became more radiant and the pounding of the hooves as I approached thundered in rhythm to the beating of my heart.

When I awoke, I gently told her it was over. She knew I wasn't kidding. She cried and so did I. But I moved out that same day.

I had a lot of ground to make up.

## Waking the Dead

It was a cold, windy afternoon in October, and my fellow writer-conspirators — Virginia, Diane, John — and I were sneaking around the Mount Pleasant cemetery in search of some inspiration.

The fall winds were blowing the leaves off the trees, laying bare the bones in anticipation of the hoary frost to come.

The grounds were mostly empty, (not the ground, though), and we toured the headstones looking for names of note and those of other centuries.

A car rolled by, driven a bit erratically by a tear-streaked woman. She must have been visiting a loved one, and had had to tear herself away as the day was fading.

Another headstone, another mausoleum.

Suddenly her car came back in the opposite direction, faster this time. We joked that she must have missed her host faster than planned. She disappeared around the corner at a pretty good clip.

Another monument, another cenotaph.

Again the car came, racing back at a high rate of speed, weaving all over the pavement. She was now crying uncontrollably, and in terror, as if being chased by the very ghost she had come to see. Her engine made enough noise to wake the dead.

It was as if the West gates of the cemetery had been locked and there were only minutes until the East gates were as well — sealing her in with the dead and possibly the undead for the night.

We stopped and locked eyes ourselves for a heartbeat. Then we started running for the car. And suddenly, we were the ones racing wild-eyed towards the exit.

The screeching tires, the busting glass... No, just the screeching of tires, as we reached the gates. And yes, there was a heavy chain imprisoning us for the night.

We scratched our collective heads, said a silent prayer and then opened the trunk. Inside was a hatchet from a camping trip.

'Lizzie Borden took an axe, and gave her mother forty whacks' seemed apropos, and so we put that poem into action immediately, making our getaway post haste.

## The Magical Cat

Copywriters: Are they born or trained? And can they be toilet trained? Is it nature or nurture? Is it in your genes or in your experience?

In the advertising business, everybody knows that account people, art directors and media buyers graduate from university. But great copywriters just crawl out of the woodwork. They either have it or they don't.

And they aren't necessarily all brainiacs. They are, of necessity, maniacs.

They are passionate. They are convinced they're right. Even if they aren't right, they have the ability to convince other people they're right. Although they are usually highly intelligent, it's an intelligence of an entirely different order. It's called emotional intelligence.

Emotional Intelligence. Copywriters are not simply presenting a logical argument that an Engineer or Scientist would respond to. They are presenting a passionate argument that appeals emotionally, intellectually and from a common-sense point of view to the Target Group they are addressing - in order to trigger a response and an action of some kind - whether it be a phone call, a visit to a website or a purchase in a store or online.

As a copywriter, you are expected to believe in the work you do and the work you present. As a copywriter, you are usually expected to tell the truth.

Sound funny? Nobody knows it, but this is your greatest asset. There is always an aspect about a product that represents something of value to the Target Group - or your client would not be in business.

In fact, they say that the worst thing for a bad product is good advertising, because, since the advertising is effective, the public will put them out of business all the faster.

And you don't need a PhD to sell a mechanic. You just need to understand the needs of a mechanic. So if you are a mechanic with a way with words, you're far better off talking to this group than somebody with a PhD who doesn't know how to turn a wrench.

If, on the other hand, you do have a PhD and a way with words, you are the ideal person to be talking to people with Masters Degrees or PhDs.

This is the beauty of it: whatever your personal life experiences, there is a market worth many millions or hundreds of millions of dollars which you can mine.

How much money is the automotive market worth worldwide? How much money is high tech engineering worth worldwide? How much money is the restaurant business in your town or city worth? What about the healthcare industry?

They need menus. They need ads. They need radio commercials. They need TV commercials. They need websites. The most probable person to write all of these materials is you, once you understand those businesses - or come from them - and assuming you have a way with words.

It might be that you've worked in that industry. It might be that you've done some research on the internet. It might be that you had a thirty-minute telephone conversation with the client.

Here's a quote from Rudyard Kipling on what to ask them:

*I keep six honest serving-men*
*(They taught me all I knew);*
*Their names are What and Why and When*
*And How and Where and Who.*

Another powerful technique is to stop thinking.

I'll tell you a technique I use to develop the ideas, and it's the exact opposite of what one might imagine would be required:

Most people think that they have to sit and think and research and scratch their heads and pound out thoughts on the keyboard, and then think some more, only to delete everything.

Then they have to do it over and over and over again, maybe for as much as a week - until they have proven to themselves why they deserve to have had a great idea through all their blood, sweat and tears.

Nothing could be further from the truth.

Here is a technique I have used my entire career to develop breakthrough ideas, and I have never read it nor heard it nor seen it anywhere. I simply ask The Magical Cat.

That name is not an accident. It's based on a dream I had before I got into the business:

*I am in a living room. A courier comes to the door with an Advertising Copywriting Project. I receive the package and go to the bedroom door. I knock, and the door opens. A Magical Cat has answered.*

*I give the Magical Cat the package, and he closes the door. Ten minutes later he comes out with a dozen amazing ideas, and the copy all in place. I thank him, and he goes back into his retreat.*

What this dream is indicating is that the most powerful creative work comes from the unconscious, not to be manipulated by you - other than to see how it fits into the requirements of the project: strategically, budget-wise, from a tone & manner point of view, and subject to client feedback.

Some editing will be required, but that's easy.

In fact, as one of the world's foremost leading philosopher/psychiatrists, Carl Jung essentially had this to say about advertising: when advertising people use eternal symbols to promote their products, they themselves are being used to disseminate the underlying reality of these symbols, helping to evolve consciousness.

From that perspective, the idea is using *you*!

# Three Strikes

It's not easy being the one who gets left out.

Somehow when kids in the neighborhood were picking players for a baseball game, I was always one of the last.

It's bad enough being stuck in left field, but when they tell you to take your glove and wait in the bleachers in case there's a foul ball, you've got a serious public relations issue.

I tried to join an actual peewee league, but they were playing hardball. He may have only been ten years old. But the pitcher's fastball reached such a velocity, I was still waiting for him to throw it after the umpire had already called a strike.

After begging my father to let me get a dog, the moment I took him off the leash, he ran away and I never saw him again.

When everybody else was playing Spin the Bottle, I was pretending to be asleep under the dining room table. I hadn't yet learned to put a lampshade on my head.

Or the time I wasn't invited to Sharon Oslander's 7th birthday party, even though everybody else in the neighborhood was.

So, when I trudged in the front door one snowy day and there was an envelope on the floor with muddy footprints on it, it was just one more example of how everybody else was the best of friends, while I was out in the cold.

And they took it for granted too, not even deigning to pick it up and open it. Every day that envelope was there getting dirtier and dirtier was a day my anger at it grew. Over the course of a week, I came to despise it, now ripped and wet from all the foot traffic, but still taunting me nonetheless.

I finally put it out of my mind entirely out of self-preservation. Until my dad walked in one day and said it was for me.

Sure enough, my name was on it. And I opened it to discover a beautiful hand-drawn invitation to Sharon Oslander's 7th birthday party, scheduled for that very day!

Just then the phone rang. It was her mother, inquiring as to why I wasn't there. Mine said it was too late to impose, but I pleaded to go and she relented. 'First, a bath!' she said, but I didn't care. And an hour later I was eating cake and ice cream.

We even played Spin the Bottle, when nobody was watching. That's when I closed my eyes and kissed Sharon herself. She didn't even wipe it off!

# Steak & Eggs, Please

I've had a few tricks played on me too, you know. There was the time someone in Grade 5 offered me a bar of Ex Lax and told me it was Swiss chocolate just before what was to be a very long walk home.

Or the car full of university students who pulled over when I was hitchhiking and rolled down the window. When I walked over to tell them where I was going, they pulled out a giant SuperSoaker water gun and drenched me from head to foot. So I could be excused for getting in a few licks of my own, especially at 20 years of age and fresh off the oil rigs.

Now it could have been the time of night or it could have been the magic mushrooms, but by the time Mark and I strolled into Denny's, we were so hungry our belly buttons were hooked to our spines. It was 3 o'clock in the dead of night, but I ordered steak and eggs, sunny side up, anyway.

It could have been the time on the clock or it could have been the magic mushrooms, but forever and a day passed with no steak and no eggs. After several entreaties to the waitress that bordered on outright begging, I finally asked to get it to go.

The waitress said Denny's didn't make steak and eggs to go, so I asked for a styrofoam container to put it in. But she said Denny's didn't have any of those either. Further investigation did reveal that Denny's did have oversized serviettes in the back though, so a few minutes later I found myself walking back to the car with my steak and eggs smirking back at me from this flimsy makeshift paper plate.

We got in the car and turned onto 82$^{nd}$ Avenue at a good clip, giving new meaning to the term 'fast food'. It began to rain, droplets the size of quarters hitting the windshield with a splat. After a couple of minutes the steak and eggs staring at me from the serviette on the palm of my hand began to weigh on me, made heavier by the realization that it was impossible to eat while underway and that the yolks could rupture at any moment.

I asked Mark what we should do with them, just as a taxi passed us on the left. We chatted for no good reason about whether football players ever become cab drivers when their careers flag.

I proposed a test. 'Well,' I said. 'Let's say we pass him and throw the steak and eggs at his windshield'. Mark looked intrigued. 'If he chases us, he's a failed football player. If he doesn't, he isn't!'

It seemed like an idea harebrained enough for the circumstances, and he was driving at a snail's pace because of the hour and the rain, so Mark stepped on the gas. As I rolled down the window, we passed the cab and I threw a perfect curveball, hitting the safety glass, the yolks congealing in the cold rain as they were smeared by the wipers clear across the windshield for a few moments. We couldn't believe our precision timing.

Suddenly the cab roared to life. 'He's a football player, Mark! Step on it!!!' But Mark was laughing so hard he couldn't press the accelerator. To avoid being tackled to death, we turned a corner, pulled over, hit the lights and sunk low in our seats, just before he flew by.

For the next 20 minutes we watched in a stupor as the cab sped past us on the cross streets, until it made a frenzied disappearance in the distance.

# Creative Integrity

Actually, it *is* all about you.

As a copywriter, if you do good work – and that can be evaluated as a combination of what you feel inside and what the industry and society at large considers it to be – you will love what you do. But this is a very subtle matter.

David Ogilvy, grandfather of modern advertising, once said, to paraphrase: 'advertising is the only industry that I know of where one can meet a copywriter who is very good. Then you meet him or her 10 years later, and they are much worse than they used to be.'

That's because these writers have been beaten down by their clients to the point where they never offer new ideas, and actually stop having them. They're doing what they think their clients expect. The trick is:

to give your client what he or she expects in a number of different executions (say 3)

to give your client what he or she needs in your view in a number of different executions (say 3)

to give your client a few more concepts that push the envelope (say 3)

to give your client a few concepts that you adore and that are good for your portfolio and the award shows (say 3)

So your client just got 12 headlines. It may not seem like much, but they are the ideas that drive the ad, that is 10 times what you're copywriting fee was, no matter what medium it is in. That ad drives the media buy, which is 10 times the revenue that the ad production was. This means that your fee only accounts for 1% of the revenue that the agency, design firm or promotions company receives.

Without your copywriting, they have nothing to present. That is why they will pay. It's not worth it for them not to do it. But please do be polite. They won't stand for arrogance, beyond a certain degree. They do expect it to some point – they need to know that you believe in what you do. But they won't be insulted.

There are really three clients here:

1) Your portfolio: If you don't do outstanding work, you're not going to progress as quickly as you want, so it's critical that you do it.
2) Your client: You want your work to serve the best interests of your client. If not, you won't have a client.
3) What your client thinks he/she wants. Your client has preconceptions; they often subscribe to the theory 'my mind is made up, please don't confuse me with facts.'

The way to resolve this conundrum is to generate enough ideas that all three of these perspectives are being addressed. Say two ideas that are on-strategy for your portfolio, three ideas that are on-strategy to serve your client's interests, and three ideas that represent what your client thinks he/she wants.

Because you want the very best work for your portfolio to be produced, a trick is to spend more of your time for the same money on ideas or clients that promote it, while quickly doing projects that generate more revenue but are not creatively satisfying.

There is a joke in the business: 'First I'll give you what you need. If you don't buy that, I'll simply give you what you want.' Another one is: 'You want to build the best possible house. Your client wants a crooked house. So your job is to build the best crooked house you possibly can.'

# My Debut on the Shirley Show

I was tricked into doing it. A Producer friend of mine talked me into appearing on The Shirley Show on a panel with Dr. Dan Kiley, author of The Peter Pan Syndrome: Men Who Have Never Grown Up.

'We want a man's perspective,' she lied. I didn't know it when I agreed, but I was being set up. It started in the Green Room, where Shirley herself pounced on me with a series of leading questions:
'How many women have you led on, then left?'
'How many times have you almost got married?'
'Do you consider women to simply exist for your own gratification?'

After sizing up the lay of the land, I told Shirley point blank: 'My fiancée, Virginia, is in the audience. I adore her — and if you ask her any questions, I'm going to give you a few choice words and walk off the show on National Television.'

The clock was ticking, so she had to agree.

I was introduced to the viewing audience as a Peter Pan. The poor sucker beside me swore under his breath and said they had been pinning him to the wall, without giving him a chance to say anything.

That's how I was forced to take up the banner.

When Shirley and Kiley started playing to the women in the viewing audience, I let Kiley have it, with such gems of insight as:

'Look, some women think they've bought and sold you just because you spent the night.'

'They wake up and make breakfast and at the table they think you're just like Daddy. And pretty soon you start acting like him.'

'Maybe these Peter Pans just wanted to wait for a woman they were actually in love with.'

'Carl Jung said that marriage was often an unwritten contract between a woman and her mother. Their men have almost nothing to do with it.'

'I can't tell you how many men I've seen being led to the altar like a lamb to slaughter, knees knocking, hands trembling, wondering how they got there with a woman they had no feelings for.'

Kiley was getting the worst of it and he pleaded silently with Shirley to intercede. She began to circle around my fiancée to see if she could use her as a cat's paw to vanquish me.

I pretended to get up and leave, so she relented.

With a sigh Kiley turned to me and shrugged. 'Okay, okay! You're right. Not all men. Just a few of them...'

When I got home, I immediately had calls of support from misunderstood men I knew everywhere.

Kiley divorced twice. And recently, my wife, Virginia, and I just celebrated our 30th wedding anniversary.

# You're in the Army Now

*Left, right! Left, right! Left, right! Left, right!*
*I had a wife with 48 kids, so I left, right! Left, right?*

It was as good a marching song as any, but who knows why anybody joins the Army? In my case, it was quite straight-forward. I'd been arrested for dealing pot out of the back of a Cadillac, owned by the father of a friend.

And my parents would only pay for the lawyer if I cut my hair and joined the Royal Hamilton Light Infantry Militia for eight weeks to straighten me out. So every day we marched around the Lieutenant-Colonel John Weir Foote Armory, learned how to assemble a rifle and shoot people, stab adversaries, kill them with hand grenades and booby traps and perform other acts of uncommon valor and service. It was grueling, but the LSD helped a lot.

Then there was the two weeks of boot camp at Petawawa on the Ottawa River. We learned how to get out of bed at Reveille, shine our shoes, make our beds, engage in target practice and cut our feet with bayonets when the Officers weren't looking to avoid marching 35 miles a day. I was the best machine gunner in the platoon, likely because my slight hand tremors compensated for the gun jerking.

The food was awful but the company was good. Some of the poor buggers didn't come back though. Our friend, Simon, drowned in the river one night after getting high. We heard a Private First Class shot himself in the mouth one day, whether by accident or design. They said I had strong leadership qualities, but didn't seem to take any of it seriously. When we got home again there was a big parade to show the colors, and it was all over. Some of us decided to join up as a career and an alternative to the steel mills. I quit school, hitchhiked out West and grew my hair again instead.

## Gambling in Macao

The 10,500,000-square-foot Venetian Macao houses a casino without parallel in the world, with no expense spared in the pursuit of opulence and grandeur. But this is a trick of the heart.

Certainly, any similar establishment would be filled with the echoes of exhilaration and conviviality, the laughter ringing out as players play to slake their passions, and wiser ones play them on their way to perdition.

But not in Macao.

In Macao, there is little drinking, carousing, gluttony or debauchery. Just the quiet, unswerving concentration of the dedicated to the very, very serious business of gambling.

This is where fortunes are lost, not heads. Men have gambled away their wives and their children at the whim of Lady Luck here, and accepted the consequences without flinching.

For in Macao, one doesn't gamble to live. One lives to gamble

# How to Quit Smoking

How to Quit Smoking.
Just when you're about to get one out of the pack, do nothing.
Just when you're about to pick up the lighter, do nothing.
Just when you feel those familiar pangs in your guts, do nothing.
Just when your hands get clammy, your throat constricts and your head feels like a watermelon with the seeds sucked out, do nothing.
Just when the room and your stomach are spinning away from you & down the toilet, do nothing.
Just when you're about to tell your coworkers to take a long jump off a short pier and your boss to commit Hari-kari, do nothing.
Just when you think you'd rather have a smoke than a massage by 18 Vestal Virgins & they work right next door, do nothing.
Just when all your friends buy Minivans, Mixmasters and electric lawn mowers, do nothing.
Just when Donald Trump wins a second term, do nothing.
Just when you're in the middle of a Night of the Living Dead, do nothing.
Just when the earth trembles & the mountains tumble into the sea, do nothing.
Just when the Klingons enslave the Federation & send its inhabitants to become fodder for abattoirs on the exoplanet Taphao Thong, do nothing.
Just when you understand that the Universe is fundamentally vacuous, do nothing.
Because it's just your body detoxing. And all you have to do is absolutely nothing.

# A Crash Course in Arctic Aviation

A Crash Course in Arctic Aviation.
*CNN, Nov 16, 2020: In an unusual collision, an airplane killed a grizzly bear while landing at the Yakutat Airport in Alaska on Saturday. Alaska Airlines Flight 66 was arriving from Cordova into Yakutat, when the captain felt an impact on the left side of the plane. Pilots then spotted the large bear lying dead, several feet off the center of the runway.*

They don't have the same respect for flying in the Arctic as they do everywhere else. They approach it more like wrangling a wild horse on the rodeo circuit than anything remotely resembling controlled mastery in the air.

The difference is obvious the moment you fly over the water and past the mountains into Iqaluit, formerly known as Frobisher Bay.

If you make it past the mountains, that is.

It's not reassuring to gaze out the window to see the dozen or so mangled carcasses of aircraft gone by, littering the mountainside just outside of town. For some inexplicable reason, for a half century or more, pilots have been overcome by the urge to turn to the right into the rock face instead of left over the bay.

It's hard to tell who was flying in and who was flying out. Or planning to, at least.

The best antidote is to join the crew in a shot of whiskey, close your eyes and grit your teeth as you are buffeted by the winds, the snow and the odd blizzard.
Crash Date: Feb 14, 1956

Aircraft: Douglas C-47 Skytrain (DC-3)
Fort Chimo Mountains

Crash Date: Sep 26, 1956
Aircraft: Avro 685 York
Fort Chimo Mountains

Crash Date: Apr 9, 1964
Aircraft: Noorduyn Norseman
Baffin Island

Crash Date: Dec 10, 1971
Aircraft: Beechcraft 80 Queen Air
Baffin Island

Crash Date: Feb 12, 1973
Type of aircraft: Douglas C-47 Skytrain (DC-3)
Frobisher Bay

Cape Dorset is renowned the world over for its remarkable Inuit soapstone carvings — and I was flying in to do a thermographic analysis of the heat loss in government buildings.

20 liters of liquid nitrogen sat at my feet for the heat-sensing camera. It turns from a gas at a frosty -196°C and the canister can't be sealed, so you don't want to knock it over. Like when there's a quick change in altitude.

Unfortunately there was a blizzard blowing at the airport, and the pilots could see virtually nothing until the last moment. When they started to land, they realized they were coming in perpendicular to the runway.

'Do you think we can do it?' one said casually. 'It's too late now,' said the other. A little Screech imported from The Rock goes a long way up there.

As we hit what passed for the tarmac, the plane bounced a few times, jerked around and skidded to a full stop. I was holding onto the nitrogen canister as if my life hung in the balance. Which it did.

Crash Date: Feb 27, 1974
Aircraft: Rockwell Sabreliner 40
Baffin Island
Crash Date: Nov 3, 1975
Aircraft: Douglas C-47A-10-DL Dakota
Frobisher Bay

Crash Date: Aug 23, 1978
Aircraft: De Havilland DHC-6 Twin Otter
Baffin Island

Crash Date: Aug 29, 1979
Aircraft: De Havilland DHC-6 Twin Otter

Baffin Island
Crash Date: Aug 5, 1990
Aircraft: Rockwell Turbo Commander
Frobisher Bay

Prince Charles once graciously called Frobisher Bay 'The Garbage Dump of the North'. But to the North and East on the way to Greenland lies Pangnirtung. With its jagged, icy peaks — the highest in the Canadian Shield — glacial lakes and summer flowers, it's why Pang is known as 'The Switzerland of the Arctic.'

I hitched a ride on a cargo plane and was told they'd put me on a return flight with a load of frozen salmon. I wondered why there were no seats until I saw exactly how much frozen salmon there were.

The plane was stacked to the gills with at least five tons of boxes, leaving virtually no room for me. When I inquired about it, the crew told me to spread-eagle on top of the cargo and hang on.

I squeezed myself between the fish and the top of the cabin with six inches to spare, gripping the salmon with white knuckles.

They fired up the engines and we trundled down the runway, but hardly at breakneck speed. Suddenly the mountain in front of us didn't look so picturesque. We were overloaded and the rock face was lunging up to block our take-off.

This may be a case of what happens in Pang really does stay in Pang.

'Are we going to make it?' the copilot asked with some trepidation. 'I don't know,' the pilot responded not so reassuringly.

But just as quickly as we needed to be, we were up and away, the load straining and creaking in its restraints. All that was left was the landing yet to come.

Crash Date: Oct 30, 1991
Aircraft:  Lockheed C-130 Hercules
Alert Bay

Crash Date: Mar 6, 1993
Aircraft: De Havilland DHC-6 Twin Otter
Baffin Island

Crash Date: Jun 20, 1996
Type of aircraft: Swearingen SA226T Merlin
Whale Cove

Crash Date: Aug 14, 1996
Aircraft: Canadian Air Force CF-18 fighter
Iqaluit Airport

Crash Date: December 3, 1998
Aircraft:          Hawker          Sidley          HS-748-2A
Iqaluit Airport

An excursion to the nether regions is guaranteed to stop any other vacation cold. And certainly the Grand Tour can be quite stimulating when conducted from the air. But you may want to enjoy the adventure in a more leisurely fashion, say from the deck of a cruise ship, plodding though that may be.

For my part, next time I'm going to take a hint from the Canada geese and fly South instead.
Crash Date: Dec 1, 1998
Aircraft: Hawker Sidley
Pond Inlet

Crash Date: Dec 3, 1998
Aircraft: Avro 748
Iqaluit

Crash Date: Dec 13, 2008
Type of aircraft: Dornier DO228
Cambridge Bay
Crash Date: May 10, 2010
Type of aircraft: De Havilland DHC-6 Twin Otter
Alert Bay Airport

Crash Date: Jul 18, 2010
Aircraft: Rockwell Aero Commander 500
Resolute Bay

# How to Act like a Film Director

It's really easy, actually. All you have to do is hire a lot of people that know much more about what you're doing than you do.

Then you really only have to answer a lot of Yes or No Questions, without revealing your ignorance.

The odd 'What do you think?' is good, if you don't understand the question at all.

Here's what you may face:

1. Did you get the money? Yes_____ No_____
2. Did you blow it? Yes_____ No_____
3. Do you like the script? Yes_____ No_____
4. Should we do it anyway? Yes_____ No_____
5. Isn't the actress too old? Yes_____ No_____
6. Do you like her tank top? Yes_____ No_____
7. Are you okay? You don't look well. Yes_____ No_____
8. Do you like her pantaloons? Yes_____ No_____
9. Do you like this prop? Yes_____ No_____
10. Is this your first time directing? Don't Answer!!!
11. Do you like this location? Yes_____ No_____
12. Do you like this set? Yes_____ No_____
13. Do we need a crane? Yes_____ No_____
14. Do you speak English? Yes_____ No_____
15. Do you like this lens? Yes_____ No_____
16. Do you like this framing? Yes_____ No_____
17. Do you like the dolly shot? Yes_____ No_____
18. Should we call the animal handler? Yes_____ No_____

19. Do you always vomit after every take? Yes_____ No_____

20. Can we just fix this in post? Yes_____ No_____

21. Do you like my characterization? Yes_____ No_____

22. Can we bring in more flibber-jabbers? Yes_____ No_____

23. Do we need another Porsche 911? Yes_____ No_____

24. Is the monster scary enough? Yes_____ No_____

25. Do you think we should call 911? Yes_____ No_____

26. Is there going to be a strike? Yes_____ No_____

27. Should we bring in the chopper? Yes_____ No_____

28. Do we want to trigger the confetti? Yes_____ No_____

29. Can we light the set on fire now? Yes_____ No_____

30. Is this MOS? I forgot to hit Record. Yes_____ No_____

31. Are the sound levels good now? Yes_____ No_____

32. Why are we working on this? Yes_____ No_____

33. Can we run the shot backwards? Yes_____ No_____

34. Do you really like the cut that way? Yes_____ No_____

35. Do you like the sepia effect? Yes_____ No_____

36. Should we fire the singer? Yes_____ No_____

37. Do you like the animation bit? Yes_____ No_____

38. Are you taking a writing credit too? Yes_____ No_____

39. Is the wrap party tonight? Yes_____ No_____

If you hired the best people, it'll be great. If you didn't, it'll look like shit.

Confer with each of the key people privately in hushed tones and always finish with a joke that elicits a loud laugh from both of you. But not at anybody's expense or they'll sabotage you.

Try to get everything in one take, then do a safety.

Keep the client away from the camera.

Make sure you point a lot during the shoot as if it's actually really important.

Kiss your DP's ass as long as he knows you'd fire him in a nanosecond if he flashes it.

Treat your Production Designer like she's your favorite pet.

Scratch your head sometimes. Look enraged here and there, but never at the talent or they'll fall to pieces.

Leave the Editor alone to demonstrate what a genius he is and why he should replace you.

Remember to take the credit for everything while complimenting everybody. Practice giving interviews in the mirror.

Throw a party and invite everybody, but act like they simply showed up.

Give an extremely arrogant yet very humble speech. Pretend you're drunk, but remember everything anybody said.

# Ulysses

*I was named by my father after his favorite poem, and once I finally read it, everything fell into place. I think he knew he was going to send me traveling by giving me away as an infant — which he did — to be recovered six months later at the urging of my mother:*
*by Lord Tennyson*

It little profits that an idle king,
By this still hearth, among these barren crags,
Match'd with an aged wife, I mete and dole
Unequal laws unto a savage race,
That hoard, and sleep, and feed, and know not me.
I cannot rest from travel: I will drink
Life to the lees: All times I have enjoy'd
Greatly, have suffer'd greatly, both with those
That loved me, and alone, on shore, and when
Thro' scudding drifts the rainy Hyades

Vext the dim sea: I am become a name;
For always roaming with a hungry heart

Much have I seen and known; cities of men
And manners, climates, councils, governments,
Myself not least, but honour'd of them all;
And drunk delight of battle with my peers,
Far on the ringing plains of windy Troy.

I am a part of all that I have met;

Yet all experience is an arch wherethro'
Gleams that untravell'd world whose margin fades
For ever and forever when I move.

How dull it is to pause, to make an end,
To rust unburnish'd, not to shine in use!
As tho' to breathe were life! Life piled on life
Were all too little, and of one to me
Little remains: but every hour is saved
From that eternal silence, something more,
A bringer of new things; and vile it were
For some three suns to store and hoard myself,
And this gray spirit yearning in desire
To follow knowledge like a sinking star,
Beyond the utmost bound of human thought.

This is my son, mine own Telemachus,
To whom I leave the sceptre and the isle,—
Well-loved of me, discerning to fulfil
This labour, by slow prudence to make mild
A rugged people, and thro' soft degrees
Subdue them to the useful and the good.
Most blameless is he, centred in the sphere
Of common duties, decent not to fail
In offices of tenderness, and pay
Meet adoration to my household gods,
When I am gone. He works his work, I mine.

There lies the port; the vessel puffs her sail:
There gloom the dark, broad seas. My mariners,
Souls that have toil'd, and wrought, and thought with
me—
That ever with a frolic welcome took

The thunder and the sunshine, and opposed
Free hearts, free foreheads—you and I are old;
Old age hath yet his honour and his toil;
Death closes all: but something ere the end,
Some work of noble note, may yet be done,
Not unbecoming men that strove with Gods.
The lights begin to twinkle from the rocks:
The long day wanes: the slow moon climbs: the deep
Moans round with many voices.

Come, my friends,
'T is not too late to seek a newer world.
Push off, and sitting well in order smite
The sounding furrows; for my purpose holds
To sail beyond the sunset, and the baths
Of all the western stars, until I die.
It may be that the gulfs will wash us down:
It may be we shall touch the Happy Isles,
And see the great Achilles, whom we knew.
Tho' much is taken, much abides; and tho'
We are not now that strength which in old days

Moved earth and heaven, that which we are, we are;
One equal temper of heroic hearts,
Made weak by time and fate, but strong in will
To strive, to seek, to find, and not to yield

## Affirmations for Donald J. Trump

1. I don't think anyone has really appreciated how truly amazing you are.
2. You have an incredible amount of ability, even when you don't use any of it.
3. Secretly, people really admire you. They're just jealous.
4. Deep down, you're actually a very nice person.
5. You're very industrious, even when you're just thinking about it.
6. People are always talking about you. When they're not, you are still probably foremost in their minds.
7. If you weren't hiding it so effectively, you'd be quite good looking.
8. If they weren't so busy, people would love to spend more time with you.
9. What you say astonishes people. That's why they don't say anything back.
10. No, you are not fat.
11. You have not been fully understood because you are ahead of your time.
12. You are a genius of unparalleled magnitude.
13. One of the most remarkable things about you is your hair.
14. You really should be appointed for life.
15. Suburban women have the hots for you.
16. It's obvious that you won.

## The Midas Touch

Sometimes the only thing more unsatisfying than failing at a long-cherished goal is succeeding at it.

Such was the experience of winning Best of Show at the Bessies, Canada's premier TV commercial gala for the advertising creative community.

As a writer, having assailed and broken through to the industry's top tier of ad agencies — and with a bagful of awards for the effort — the only remaining task was to reach for the highest honour.

We knew we had a shot at a prize because of the uniqueness of the creative.

But when the organizers put us at a table near the front, we were confused, since we weren't friends with the judges or anything of the sort.

The Master of Ceremonies plodded though the awards category by category until all that was left was the big three.

We didn't win the Bronze. "Must be a pal of the Committee," my Creative Director groused.

We didn't win the Silver. "The whole thing is fixed," lamented my Art Director.

As the drum roll started for the Best of Show, it hit me: "No, we're going to get the top prize!"

Sure enough, we did. And after the speeches and all the hoopla, we went down to the hotel bar to receive the accolades of our mates and a late night of celebration. But there were no accolades and no celebrations.

As they wandered in to really tie one on, the crowds gathered unto themselves, free to complain about the unfairness of it all and share the latest conspiratorial gossip.

Nobody said even a word to us. Recognizing the vulnerability of our position, my Creative Director bolted for the door.

My Art Director immediately took his winnings in the shapely form of a star-struck student who'd sneaked in. And I was alone to face the awful truth, that glory is its own punishment.

Fortunately, Virginia diagnosed my condition as soon as I got home and threw a celebration party to commemorate the occasion a few days later.

But the gold I had pursued so single-mindedly had already lost its lustre.

.

# Hear No Evil, Speak No Evil

I was part of a group who met once a month to share an interesting outing for discussion.

One such evening, I convened with Mario, Rob and Diane at City Hall to see the Eternal Flame lit by the Pope during his visit.

Originally, on bad advice, the Pontiff was scheduled to give his blessings from Wonder Mountain, a gaudy simulated amusement ride complete with roller coaster.

Thankfully more mature heads prevailed, and his remarks were relocated to a more stately venue.

The only proviso was that nobody in our company was allowed to speak during the entire event.

Such a caveat means the discursive mind is bypassed, enabling the subject to experience a more profound sense of being, without the chattering mind interceding with its annoying commentary on things as they unfold.

In this altered state, we took in the Flame, the Henry Moore sculpture, the fountains and more, enjoying the sanctity that nonverbal engagement can confer.

'Hey!!!' a gruff voice cried out. We turned to see a ragged-looking tough bearing down on us. 'Have you got a smoke???'

Without a word, I reached into my pocket and pulled out a pack, giving him one of the last that I had.

Rather than thanking me, he turned to Diane and made the same demand. She generously gave him three, which he snatched up quickly.

Then he turned back to me with a snarl. 'You only gave me one!' he bellowed. He seemed ready to assault me, and I blinked silently in anticipation. Suddenly he stopped in his tracks, a light dawning on his face.

'Hey, I just got out of prison — and even I wouldn't hit people like you!' Obviously he thought we were hearing and speech impaired. It seems that even in a maximum security prison, they still have some moral sensibility.

He stormed off to root out his next injustice, stopping once or twice to look back, to consider whether he had just been had.

.

## Danny Aiello & The Art of Being Real

In the back room of a trendy Yorkville restaurant we wait, the afternoon soireé abuzz and aglow with the launch contingent of 'Brooklyn Lobster', the new film by director Kevin Jordan.

The champagne flows freely, succulent plates of the king of crustaceans are everywhere. And being seriously ignored.

That's because the main course is about to arrive: Danny Aiello, star of the film and character in his own right.

The swarming of the festival is becoming almost overwhelming: The press, the publicists, the agents, the producers, the wannabes and the wish-they-coulds, not to mention the crowds throwing their necks out, trying to catch a glimpse as they strut past the French doors to the promenade.

It seems busy enough, until the crush arrives. Somehow the crowd knows five minutes in advance, must be that PDA kinda thing. The buzz becomes cacophonous, the guests all atwitter, everybody is almost famous in the wink of one's eye.

With a gust of wind and aplomb he arrives. Danny Aiello. His handlers are like coast guard cutters, parting the waters easily, and ushering him to a reserved seat at the back of the affair. He is tall, good looking, strong — so Danny.

Everything about him radiates authenticity, and for good reason. This is a man who became an actor almost by accident at the ripe age of 39, a time when many thespian careers are finished. Now at 71, he is just reaching middle age. Such are the blessings of cleaving to one's real identity.

Born in poverty in Manhattan, abandoned by his father, he sold newspapers, shined shoes and did whatever else he could to help support his struggling family. Then onto stints in the army, as a bouncer, on a bus line — even as a union president.

Onscreen, it is easy to see him in these roles and it's likely the reason his celluloid persona is so convincing. He is everyman: real, without affectation, affable, angry, witty, wry — but more than anything, genuine.

How has it been working with the likes of Francis Ford Coppola, Woody Allen, Spike Lee, Robert Altman, Norman Jewison and almost every other directorial phenomenon going? A big smile. 'I love them all,' he says with a gleam in his eye, and you just know they love him.

His role as Frank Giorgio, an aging patriarch fighting to save his family's lobster farm from foreclosure, is played with empathy and deftness. Presented by Martin Scorsese and co-starring Jane Curtin as his long-suffering wife, the film explores the journey of this somewhat dysfunctional family, as the father consistently ignores advice and stubbornly makes mistakes in the face of unrelenting change.

His discovery is that the love of those close to him defines him far better than what he has been doing in his business. It is all the more compelling because it is based on the director's personal experience growing up. According to Jordan, Aiello's participation did not leverage the production budget on its own. The director resorted to cobbling together from a wide variety of friends and acquaintances in a truly independent effort.

It subsequently attracted the attention of Scorsese, who agreed to become associated after the fact.

Full of nostalgia, 'Brooklyn Lobster' exudes everything that makes Danny Aiello special. The same humanity and unblemished heart is evident as in such exceptional productions as 'Radio Days', 'Moonstruck', 'Do The Right Thing' and over forty others.

What binds audiences the moment they see Danny Aiello on the silver screen? "I'm not sure. I seem to connect with them somehow, in a way that really affects them." Is it because — unlike many screen personas — they immediately know he is being real? A big smile steals across his face. "You know, that's it!"

Is it possible they gravitate to him because he is actually playing himself? His irresistible smile becomes even broader.

Meanwhile, the crowd is experiencing an epiphany. They had ordered a celebrity off the menu. But they were served the epitome of real life.

*Danny Aiello moved on to even greater things on December 12, 2019.*

# The Book of Fancies

## The Strike of the Super Virus

It started out innocuously enough, the first evidence becoming apparent approximately seven million years ago, mutating rapidly into its current form.

While lying relatively dormant first in the jungles of Africa, the virus reached a breakout point and started to spread elsewhere — slowly at first, then gaining momentum, growing exponentially.

Now rampant around the globe, the virus is poised to eradicate all life as we know it on the planet. It causes food diversity to collapse, water to become poisoned, the air to be unbreathable and eventually is predicted to blot out the sun or cause a nuclear catastrophe.

If the past is any indication of its virulence, it may be so contagious as to infect other solar systems and spread across the galaxy.

Fortunately, nature seems to be developing an antiviral to this plague and this blight on the health of Earth may be headed to the scrap heap of biological history.

Experts have tentatively named this natural antiviral Humanivir.

# Like Father, Like Son

It's a fall day in the cemetery, where Will Schmedlik is standing in the pouring rain, looking down on his father's headstone. Filled with angst, recalling a lifetime of insult and injury foisted upon him by his immigrant parent, motherless, poverty-stricken, a home-life bereft of caring, understanding and joy, his tears mix with the rain that is spattering on the granite. It may as well have been his own blood.

He falls to his knees crying, screaming in rage and anguish at his father. After a few minutes, he collapses to the ground into the mud in despair. As if the heavens have spent all their tears, the rain tapers off and ceases.

A finger taps him on the shoulder. Startled, Will looks up to see a priest.

"My son. My son. Lift up thine eyes," says the priest. "The past is nothing but a fleeting shadow. You cannot relive it, or change a single thing."

The priest holds out his hand to Will. "Rise - rise and greet the glory of this day. Be as if you were reborn!!!"
The priest starts to help Will up. As if he has been thrown a lifeline, he grabs the headstone and begins to stand. The headstone falls over, hitting Will on the head, and he promptly dies.

\* \* \*

Will regains consciousness in the Costume Department of a theatrical company. Surrounding him are garments, masks, props and thespian paraphernalia. Suddenly, out jumps the Wardrobe Master, a grubby little dwarf, covered in tattoos. "We're not open. Come back in the morning!" he says.

Will jumps up and steps back. The Wardrobe Master leans toward him aggressively. "Who sent you? Do you have your paperwork? Didn't they give you instructions???"

"Uh - no –" Will stutters.

"Did they at least give you a number?"

Will shakes his head.

The Wardrobe Master begins ranting, fulminating, almost foaming at the mouth. "Why don't they follow procedures? How can I get organized if they don't follow procedures???"

Will looks so alarmed, his host relents - suddenly grinning from ear to ear. "Okay, fine. What are you looking for?"
"I don't know..."

The host rolls his eyes to the heavens. "If you know who you are, the choice is easy!!!"

"I just don't know — "

"Well, what do you want then???"

"I guess I want to be...reborn — "

You've come to the right place. And believe me — the minute you came in, I had your number..."

He pulls a costume off the rack, with a flourish and shows it off proudly. "Hamlet! He couldn't decide who he was either." Then in a British accent: "To be or not to be...I think you're not to be, based on what I see — " Will steps back. The Master sneers and tosses the costume. "Picky, picky, picky! Fine - since you don't know who you are...how's Marie Antoinette?" He grabs her costume, with a French accent: "Let them eat cake! Let them eat cake!

111

Let them eat cake!" He leans into Will and whispers. "I may work in Wardrobe now - but I was a star of the stage once. How I ended up here, I'll never know. But nobody ever does..."

Will starts looking for a way out of the place.

Wardrobe Master: "There's nowhere to go, you know. No matter what you do, you'll always be right here."

The Master whips out a Matador costume, unfurling the red cape in Will's face. "En Garde! I challenge you! I challenge your father! I challenge your grandfather! I challenge your grandfather's grandson! Don't be a coward!!! What a load of bull..."

When Will demurs, the Master whips out a series of costumes, now aggressively trying to sell him on one or the other. "Giacomo Casanova! She loves me. She loves me not. She loves me!!! "Confucius! But you're confused enough..."

"Einstein? Caesar?? Churchill? ?? Cleopatra? ??? General George A. Custer????? Now this is my very last stand..."
Will is so uncertain about which costume to choose, as they are being shoved in his face rapid-fire, he just can't make a decision.

The Master is becoming very aggravated. "Look, if you can't decide, we're going to be here for all eternity!"
He blinks foolishly, realizing the irony of it.

Then he recovers. "Time's up — I'll just give you one off the rack. They've all been marked down anyway!'
Aghast, Will recognizes his own father's garments.
In 1932, in a cabin outside Druzhny, Belarus, Will Schmedlik was reborn as his very own father. His mother died in childbirth.

# The Roach Motel

It was a chilly, Fall evening in the autumn of my life, the rain spattering on my cracked windshield, playing havoc with its incessant drumbeats on the decaying maple leaves plastered hodge-podge on the glass, while all the while the road continued rolling on relentlessly in an excruciatingly aggravating manner in perfect synchronization to the monotony of this inexcusable run-on sentence.

I took a very short break from the computer for a well-deserved rest, and drew another suspense-laden breath. Just at that very moment, the most welcome sight greeted my timeworn eyes and my overtaxed neocortex. I beheld a place to sleep, perchance even to dream of faraway snores: The Roach Motel.

It lurched out of the looming landscape like a little old lady who had languished long past the luscious, licentious but lonely life she had lived, much in the lovely way alliteration can lie on the page, enlivening the literati yet belaboring the language, being both lofty and lackluster simultaneously at the same time.

Making a quick decision, I turned the page and drove up the driveway. The lights were out. But the sign flickered ominously, as if choreographed by a malevolent creative miscreant whose only motivation was to add mystique and magic realism to an already burdened narrative.

I thought it was instructive – even a dead giveaway – that all the other parking spots were vacant. I just wasn't certain what it was instructing me to do. But there was a used car lot next door. I intuitively took this as a sure sign I should drive straightaway to look for other lodgings, but my sense of misadventure and predilection for misdirection drew me hypnotically like iron filings to a magnet towards the Roach Motel Office.

I tried the door but it was locked. I knocked on it several times to no answer. I tapped on the window, I rang the buzzer, I swung the hefty knocker against the heavy, vainglorious oaken obstruction.

I was about to turn and leave when the door creaked open. Peering out was a spindly old man, so frail that one might shatter his delicate constitution with a quick sneeze. 'Can I help you?' he inquired. On my asking to be put up for the night, he simply nodded and beckoned me to follow.

The room was tidy enough, but it had a strange smell about it, almost like a chemical of some sort – the kind that has been banned for decades, perhaps since the Great War.

I settled in well enough. That's when I didn't see it. A little brown blur it was, scurrying under the hotplate to avoid the light. Then another, squeezing behind the icebox. In the bathroom, there were a half dozen of them in the tub, and that's when I fled to the Office.

'Not again!' said the Manager. 'We'll have to call The Exterminator. But don't worry, he lives just up the road.' Sure enough, one quick phone call, and his truck rolled up a few minutes later. There was a lot of clattering and banging as all the equipment came out and he brought it through the front door.

In front of my eyes was a 6'5" cockroach with his coveralls on, staring down at me. The Manager pointed at me and said: 'We've got another customer, Bob.' I was exterminated a very short time later and the Manager relocated my vehicle to the used car lot next door.

So if you ever come across the Roach Motel, just keep on driving. Because people check in. But they don't check out.

# Download Situation Report

The User thought he was downloading Microsoft Office 2019 after paying for it. But it was only Microsoft Office 2010. He was going to use it for his new laptop. But he put it on his desktop out of reflex, prompted by Mind Program IV.

As predicted, he decided to transfer the software. But he couldn't find it on his desktop when he looked for the download. As called for by Protocol 35180P, it disintegrated immediately subsequent to download.

He decided to keep using his existing Microsoft Office 2007, and to migrate a version to the laptop. But he noticed it had no DVD slot, and of course, no mouse.

As expected, he gave up and purchased Microsoft Office365 for installation directly onto the portable. He couldn't disable the laptop's access password at first, but after a number of ingenious attempts, he was able to circumvent it.

He had paid again, and received the 365 link, but had to register with our Microsoft Gatekeeper to go any further, since he didn't have an account. Our plan was working.

It didn't accept the information, of course, and after 2 attempts Our Section Leader locked him out. But it did direct him to access a Telephone Code, supposedly for security reasons.

When he called for the Code, he was correctly told that Our Section Leader sent him a text message with the information. But, congruent with our examinations, his landline doesn't receive texts.

Meanwhile, the Norton security software that had been insinuated into his laptop by our Team prior to its acquisition buried a new password he generated in the Security Vault and substituted another one. He couldn't use it because of its inherent conflict.

He called our agents at Microsoft Customer Service but, of course, nobody answered.

After that, he had a long online chat with a Microsoft Customer Service expert, who turned out to be a scammer, one of our 'moles.' He didn't know it until he was asked for five bucks.

Our Section Leader then sent him a video on how to install Microsoft Office365. But it was 10 minutes long and we knew he was toggling between two computers, one having no mouse, and he was teetering on the edge of a meltdown.

What's more, our video narrator was programmed to sound as though he was born in Borneo. It was unintelligible to the Subject Target.

He was ready for harvesting.

He tried using the video to escape the trap for 18 minutes until his brain short-circuited. That's when he blacked out and he is now comatose.

Please advise Mother Ship the Subject is now ready for collection and reprogramming. Excellent work, Team! Your collective Good Spirit will be reported to The Great Cyber Leader hovering in the sky.

# The Book of Ancestors

# The Munro Clan:
## From the Romans to the Vikings

*Genealogy (Excerpt), Robert Morris Munroe, 1931*
The origin of the clan Munro is lost in that legendary obscurity which is the sure proof of real antiquity.

Sir Robert Douglas states that the family, one of the most ancient, was driven over to Ireland by the Romans in the year 357, and that only after sojourning there 700 years did it return to its original Highland home. The clan exhibited a purely Gaelic origin, it having been driven down into the Southern Highlands from the rocky Highlands of the North. However, one fact emerges: 'The Founder of the family, the first Munro who held land, was a certain Donald.'

Donald received from Malcolm the 2nd for aid given against the Danes the land on Alness Water, called Ferindonald (or Donald's land), subsequently erected into the Barony of Fowlis, and still in the possession of the family. He died in 1053, being succeeded by his son...
George, who helped Malcolm the 3rd, son of King Duncan, who wrest the Scottish throne from MacBeth between 1054 and 1057.
.
Hugh, who was created the first Baron of Fowlis. From him the title and estates came down in uninterrupted lineal male descent for nearly 800 years, which is said to be almost unexampled in the family histories of Scotland or England, and only paralleled in the succession of the Lord's Kingsale, premier Barons of Ireland.

# Castle Fowlis

*Courtesy of Clan Munro Association*
The Munros were granted Lands in Ross in the 11th
Century by a grateful King after assisting him in defeating
the Viking invaders of this part of Scotland.

From documentary evidence, they were well established
by the middle of the 14th Century on the north shore of
the Cromarty Firth in the area known as Ferindonald
(Donald's land) after their legendary first chief. From this
narrow base comprising the modern parishes of Kiltearn
and Alness they gradually spread their sphere of influence
north and eastwards into the fertile plain of Easter Ross.

Loyal to the Crown, early in the reformation the Chief and
his followers adopted the Protestant faith. Under their
Chief they fought in the 30 Years War and supported the
Protestant succession to the British Crown against the
Catholic Stuarts during the Jacobite Risings of the C18th.

The Munros military record continued into the present
century, providing the British Government with some of
its finest fighting troops through the Highland Regiments.
Clansmen and women have excelled in many professions
including medicine and politics. Military expeditions,
adventurism and social change in the Highlands saw the
name Munro spread throughout the world. The power of
the old Highland Chieftains has gone but the spirit of the
Clan lives on through the Clan Munro Association which
enjoys a world-wide membership.

Fowlis Castle itself is mentioned in records that date back
to the 14th century although the original Tower of Fowlis
was believed to have been built in 1154. It is recorded by
evidence Uilleam III, Earl of Ross granted a charter to

Robert the Munro of Fowlis for the lands of "Estirfowlys" with the "Tower of Strathskehech" from 1350.

It is also recorded that Euphemia I, Countess of Ross granted two charters to Robert's son, Hugh Munro, 9th Baron of Fowlis in 1394. A document signed and sealed at Fowlis Castle in 1491 reads in Gaelic "Caisteal biorach, nead na h-iolair", which means "castle gaunt-peaked, the eagle's nest." The lands remain in the custody of the clan.

# Newton

*Distillate, Donald Gordon Munroe, 1934*

Here in Westminster lies Isaac Newton, knight, the incomparable genius of science. He discovered the laws of gravitation, ascertained the earth's form and motion, and the course of the tides; he was also familiar with the ways of light.

Whilst pondering the integral calculus which was his own, he thought to apply it as to the Apocalypse to compute the date of the Day of Judgment. Ah! When will mathematicians learn that their method is but a grinder, which can indeed produce pork sausage from pork, but not gold dust from iron!

# Voltaire

*Distillate, Donald Gordon Munroe, 1934*

My imprudent pen sent me once into exile in
England, twice to the Bastille. Banishment and
prison completed my education so well founded by
the Abbé de Chateau Neuf, Ninon de Lenclos, my
mother's friend and the Jesuits of the College de
Louis-le-Grand.

Eventually I learned how to deride the great of this
earth, as well as very sacred things with absolute
impunity.

The formula I used is not complicated. It has but four
essentials:

*1 – Jibe only with ostentatious politeness; there is
then no risk, for the mighty never understand irony;*

*2 – Remain outside the temporal jurisdiction of those
whom you lampoon;*

*3 – Wear always a mocking smile, even though it be
hated by weaklings like Alfred de Musset;*

*4 – Remember Balthasar Gracian's
aphorism…'There is no greater empire a man can
have than over himself.'*

I have spoken.

# Goethe

*Distillate, Donald Gordon Munroe, 1934*

Here in the Asphodel  meadows, I walk each day
conversing with Homer, Virgil and Shakespeare.
Sometimes Dante joins us too. We have no flesh.
Having none, we are free from desire, and all other
ills of the body.

Although long-dead, we still concern ourselves with
certain human affairs. The Greeks and the Romans
are softened by age; they dream of mythical heroic
deeds in the far distant past; Dante muses on
Mediaeval Florence, sometimes on the ultimate
destiny of Mussolini; Shakespeare thinks of the court
of Queen Bess, occasionally of post-Victorian
England.

I consider the Germany I loved, and knew in life
when Frederick The Great was King of Prussia, and
the Grand Duke of Wiemar was my patron. It
saddens me to contemplate the present Reich
prostrate at the feet of a bombastic montebanc.

The contrast is not pleasant, but  perhaps to appraise
correctly, I should have that for which I asked with
my dying breath...*light...more light*

# Huxley

*Distillate, Donald Gordon Munroe, 1934*

Be sure, valiant invincible soul, that although the
fortuitous concourse of atoms which once was
Huxley is now physically dispersed, it will live
forever in honour and integrity in the minds of those
who profess to love truth.

# Hamilton

*Distillate, Donald Gordon Munroe, 1934*

I am Alexander Hamilton. After Aaron Burr's fatal
bullet lodge in my body, I came to Trinity
churchyard to rest, far indeed from my West Indian
birthplace in mountainous Nevis, but at home here at
the head of Wall Street.

Consistent believe in the infinite wisdom of men of
wealth, I was ever at odds with Jefferson who had an
equally fanatical confidence in the populace. He was
wrong, but so was I!

# John Henry Munroe

*Distillate, Donald Gordon Munroe, 1934*

Grandfather, although thirty years have passed since you left this life, you have still the love and affection I gave you when I was a little child.

Your strong, intelligent face is as distinct in my memory as though I had seen it yesterday.

I shall never forget your kindness and generosity, your courage in the face of difficulties, your independent spirit, your fortitude in sorrow and disaster.

Thank you, grandfather, for the example you have set, however poorly it may have been followed and wherever you are, rest in peace.

# As to Prophets & Prophecies

*One Man's Meat, Robert Morris Munroe, 1933*

The weatherman, he thus prognosticates:
'Cloudy today. Tomorrow, thunder showers.'
Then when tomorrow comes (o prankish Fates!)
the dial numbers none but sunny hours.

Next day he tries another tack. Says he:
'Continued fair with rising temperature,'
Comes rain and wind; the silly mercury
Descends, much to our friends' discomfiture.

The moral then, it seems to me, is plain:
The prophet and the guesser are as one.
Who guesses best anent Life's tangled skein
Is the best prophet, once the thread is spun.

## The Great Editor

*by Robert Morris Munroe, 1933*

Brisbane diluted! Bush-league Docfrankcrane!
This pseudo-cynic glances down his nose
At all human weakness, a pose
Midway between amusement and disdain.
From time to time he tries a humorous vein,
Deluded dunce and doubtless never knows
How dull most readers find his verse and prose;
His choicest quips give me a shooting pain.

Each paragraph a sneer, each sneer a kiss
For his own vanity, 'he tells the world'
In stuffy platitudes how he'd do this
Or that; and sees Red battle-flags unfurled.
The sleep of such a mind no thought disturbs;
He counts it clever using nouns as verbs.

## Daybreak

*By Donald Mackenzie Munroe, 1983*

Morning trembles in the pearly mist.
Soon my heart will rise
Like wild geese from the marshes.

# Postscript

*One Man's Meat, Robert Morris Munroe, 1933*
Regrets! Would you regret the crescent moon
Rising above the ocean's silver brim?
Then why regret the gift you made to him
Who reverently knelt to ask a boon
From love? Ah, you must know that all too soon
Will come the specter Old Age, stark and grim,
To slow the pulse, retard the lissome limb,
And leave but memories of our commune.

How well you know the heart has found content!
Why struggles then the mind against its fate?
No chain of reasoning can circumvent
(Much less deny) that urge importunate
And ere you pass beyond your lover's ken,
Know this: with women so it is with men.

# The Book of Spirit

# The House of Mirrors

There was a living Zen koan I was confronted with at the age of six or seven. It was always waiting for me at the barber shop, like a cat outside a mouse hole.

I loved going to the barber shop because the proprietor, Luigi, was so nice to me. Plus there was the candy — and he wasn't even a stranger. It was a substitute for conversation, since I couldn't speak much Italian.

As was his trade, he would gently trim my hair, tilting my head to one side, then the other. Similar to what I wished my father would have done, a tender touch, a few words of caring freely spoken.

But there was something more profound hidden in the shop, one that would reverberate down through the years, informing my experience. The mirror! And not just one but two, facing each other to proffer a full view of my head back and front.

But of course, in the reflection was another smaller version of the one behind me. Which contained another even smaller. And the succession of mirrors led off into the reflection of infinity, never-ending, every second one framing my own eyes.

Chills ran up my spine as I was awakening, dozens of identical eyes boring into mine, slicing through reality like a can opener and pinning my experience of life to the wall like a thumbtack.

I couldn't have articulated it then, but I was experiencing the universe as one single consciousness underlying everything. My own.

My parents wondered why I was so excited about going to Luigi's. But they must have chalked it up to the candy.

# Black Ice

I was driving through the dark while in the middle of an intense philosophical discussion with a close companion about Jung's theory that throughout the course of one's life there is an arc that proceeds from one set of traits to its opposite. In my case, for instance, from that of an Angry Young Man to a more gentle iteration.

Only through the integration of the two is the worst outcome of either avoided.

I merged from the 427 onto the 401 and that's when I didn't see it. Black Ice. But I knew it was there. And at such a speed on a sweeping curve, I executed one of the most difficult maneuvers one can in a crisis as dangerous as this. I did absolutely nothing. I said nothing and my copilot did the same. I relinquished the brakes and the accelerator. I became the human equivalent of black ice.

As the car glided around the curve, the tires had just enough traction to keep up with the momentum without sliding sideways and we hit the straightaway. Just in time to see a 4x4 spinning a full $360°$ in the lane directly beside us on the left at 70 miles an hour, propelled by centrifugal force and the panic of its occupants. Followed by a pickup doing the same in the lane on the right. It was a dance of death in slow motion, but there was just enough room to float between its jaws and off into the night.

Under those conditions, there was nothing for it but to call 911 and hope for the best. I never did hear what became of them, but it couldn't have been very pretty, what with the other vehicles coming up fast out of the darkness.

The experience was a physical enactment of Jung's theory of opposites, putting the finer point of reality on it. And we had just threaded the needle.

## Paradise Lost

In the Lesser Antilles she lies and a million light
years away. The volcano rises from the ocean floor
offering sustenance and succour to all who seek
shelter beneath her skirts.

But way down, she gets angry, seething without
reason, The fauna scatters with nowhere to hide. The
birds take flight.

Even the Stones themselves leave the refuge of the
recording studio for fresh Air.

The sky turns dark. The sea is spitting fire and
spewing poison.   Her rage boils up and over the
calderas, her pent up magmanimosity raining down
on ungulates and ingrates alike.

And Heaven falls into the stone face of the Earth, the
last piece of Paradise, lost, and the heart of it torn
asunder.

# The Question

'What is that?' I asked my parents, at the age of three.
They didn't answer.
'What is that?' I asked again with the same result.
'What is that?' I asked again with the same result.
'What is that?' I asked again with the same result.
'What is that?' I asked again with the same result.
'What is that?' I asked again with the same result.
'What is that?' I asked again with the same result.
'What is that?' I asked again with the same result.
'What is that?' I asked again with the same result.
'What is that?' I asked again with the same result.
'What is that?' I asked again with the same result.
'What is that?' I asked again with the same result.
'What is that?' I asked again with the same result.
'What is that?' I asked again with the same result.
'What is that?' I asked again with the same result.
'What is that?' I asked again with the same result.
'What is that?' I asked again with the same result.
'What is that?' I asked again with the same result.
'What is that?' I asked again with the same result.
'What is that?' I asked again with the same result.
'What is that?' I asked again with the same result.
'What is that?' I asked again with the same result.
'What is that?' I asked again with the same result.
'What is that?' I asked again with the same result.
'What is that?' I asked again with the same result.
'What is that?' I asked again with the same result.
'What is that?' I asked again with the same result.
'What is that?' I asked again with the same result.
'What is that?' I asked again with the same result.
'What is that?' I asked again with the same result.
'What is that?' I asked again with the same result.
'What is that?' I asked again with the same result.
'What is that?' I asked again with the same result.
'What is that?' I asked again with the same result.

'What is that?' I asked again with the same result.
'What is that?' I asked again with the same result.
'What is that?' I asked again with the same result.
'What is that?' I asked again with the same result.
'What is that?' I asked again with the same result.
'What is that?' I asked again with the same result.
'What is that?' I asked again with the same result.
'What is that?' I asked again with the same result.
'What is that?' I asked again with the same result.
'What is that?' I asked again with the same result.
'What is that?' I asked again with the same result.
'What is that?' I asked again with the same result.
'What is that?' I asked again with the same result.

'It's a record player,' they finally blurted out.

Their little experiment in tenacity had gone off the rails and they realized that after more than 40 inquiries, I was never going to stop without the answer.

'Where does it come from?'
'From the record player store,' they said with a sigh.

'Where does that come from?'
They rolled their eyes. 'From the record player factory.'

'Where does that come from?'
'From the construction company.'

'Where does that come from?'
'From the construction company factory'

It didn't take long for me to realize they had no idea regarding where everything was coming from. And, in fact, they didn't understand the question. Perhaps I should have been clearer.

I stopped listening after that and began to inquire elsewhere

## Untitled

There are the little events in life. And there are the significant events in life. Individually, they all seem to have their place. But what happens when we take them together as one?

A unified picture begins to emerge, much like an impressionist painting, a mandala, a lenticular image, an autostereogram, yielding up an underlying theme that sews one's experiences into a deeper narrative, rendering a profile of the myths we are living out.

It is the Rorschach analysis of our souls. And it has no name

## All True Art

...arises not by scouring the detritus of what anybody else has done, nor by agreement with the collective remains of that corpse, but by diving into the source that gives rise to these ashes and everything else. Information, knowledge, opinion — these are shadows eradicated when the light is turned on ~

# Between Heaven & Earth

To paraphrase Miyamoto Musashi in the early 17th Century, looking up at Mount Fuji: 'Compared to the mountain, I am insignificant.'

The waves of self doubt washed over him, and beneath them finally came a realization that was to change his life and make him the legendary swordsman that he was. 'How big is this mind that can carry such a mountain within it?'

Or as Jimi Hendrix had it: 'I'm standing next to a mountain. Gonna chop it down with the edge of my hand…'

Of course in our long and winding travels towards the light of understanding, we have taken many journeys as a species, and we have dispensed with limit after limit, as our outdated cosmology has caved and crumbled in the face of reality and our capacity to apprehend it.

Science, for instance, has taken us an immense distance, serving as a guide into and through the Great Unknown as it has unfolded. But it has circumscribed a fragmented and feeble perspective based on one essential fallacy: The separation of existence into inner and outer experiences.

How is it that the dimensions of length, width, height, space and time itself can be analyzed, while a perspicacious consideration of other dimensions is ignored?

Defining influences such as consciousness, awareness, attention, perspective, not to mention a nearly infinite parade of mental and emotional states — all these and more are dimensions of reality as we perceive it.

It could even be said that this artificial separation of reality into Heaven and Earth has been manufactured to obscure the uncomfortable possibility that there is no objective reality at all.

And what if this arbitrary delineation between inner and outer experiences were seen as just that?

The creeping realization that all of existence is an integrated whole might rear its enlightened head.

We might truly begin to act as stewards of the planet. We might eradicate poverty, and work even more diligently toward overcoming disease and drought and war.

We would have put the Being into the human being and Heaven and Earth would become One. To practice this is in itself a reason to have been born.

# What's Shaking

My father had a Familial Tremor.

His older brother, a world-renowned entomologist did, yet he was famous for his collection of moths and butterflies, not even dislodging the powder on their illustrious yet delicate wings.

Some of my siblings are afflicted and my paternal grandmother was also, a gentle soul so I was advised. Being a guy I was not advised to show my feelings much, so this was a way to shake it all out.

The older I got the more my hands started to tremble, especially when I became out of touch with myself, and was sucked out into the illusion of the world.

I went to a specialist who said it could be diminished through a revolutionary procedure in which connections in the brain are severed. The only side effect, I was told, was the loss of creativity.
Which happens to be the élan vital for me. Not to mention, the way I make a living. It sounded like the high-born cousin of a lobotomy, so I demurred.

Sometimes the kundalini races up my spine too fast in its mad journey to manifestation. It includes all the energy of existence and none of it — the passion, the creativity, the joy, the anger.

It rips through my flesh and my mind. Shall I go to a physician to get a prescription for the universe?

This phenomenon actually happens in the soul. It is shaking all over and it has a lot more of that to do.

# Lomi Lomi

I always liked pineapples. So juicy, tart and succulent, they explode in a burst of healthful flavor and dribble down the chin faster than you can say 'This is the closest thing to Hawaiian heaven!'

Or so I thought.

And where you find pineapples, you may find the ancient Hawaiian practice of forgiveness, Ho'oponopono.

Translated roughly into English, it is rendered as:
*I love you*
*I am sorry*
*Please forgive me*
*Thank you*

The subject of the prayer need not be present, nor even be aware of the process and the result is said to be dramatic self-healing as things real or perceived are put right.

And where you find Ho'oponopono, you'll find other, more rarefied healing regimens.

For instance, the Medicine Man may prescribe an hour or so of Lomi Lomi. Once I heard about it, I knew my soul was crying out for it, so I promptly booked an intervention.

I was taken into a consecrated sacred space by two Highly-Trained Goddess Practitioners, one to my left and one to my right. Knowing I was a neophyte, they kindly but firmly directed me to disrobe entirely.

Being somewhat modest, I elected to keep my underpants in their usual place.

My hosts also effected a ritualized state of undress themselves, and once in this condition, they proceeded to rub fine oils, sacred unguents and special perfumes — initially on my person, then on theirs.

At first, they utilized their hands. Then they brought their entire Rubenesque bodies into spiritual play, colliding with and transforming my negative energies into an enlightened state of pure joy.

It was like a Picasso painting of flesh: arms, legs, torsos thrown together into a heavenly Mix Master, the undulations set to Hawaiian guitars.

When I could think at all, it was mostly about pineapples.

After a half an hour or so, I thought I'd died and gone to Lani.

The Practitioners seemed to be enjoying it also, if their sacred heavy breathing was any indication.

All too soon it was over. It was winter out, so I grudgingly had to put my clothes on before leaving.

But I carried memories of lei and a little Hawaiian sunshine in my soul.

And a quart of the Polynesian equivalent of Mazola corn oil spread all over my body.

## Living Death

It comes in every moment and passes away.
At certain junctures in life, it is more pronounced.
The falling of dead leaves.
The seven-year cycle, the end of a relationship
a fading
a dead cat
end of a passion or a dream.
In simple cultures, and longstanding ones, there are
rituals for this
embedded in everyday life.
The more fully the experience is lived, the greater the
transformation
— breeding more life, and more authentically.
 Yet we are hypnotized into avoiding the experience,
and in that, life gets more shallow:
comparing,
competing,
blaming,
beating,
boasting,
bloating, skin-deep or less
to the fabric even.
But it can't be evaded.
Stand up and take it without moving or thinking.
Then the chrysalis falls, and onto the next.
But not prematurely, or it will not fully detach
and a lot of running around will be required.

## The Mind of a Child

In metaphysics, I have always found that when I give up my inner spirit guide in favor of someone else's direction, no matter how well intended or skillful, I seem to end up a thousand miles from where I intended to go.
And in those cases, I have had to return to the point of departure. With the mind of a curious child.
In practice, my experience is that there is fundamentally no journey at all. It is the world that moves. So nobody can instruct me on how to get anywhere.

## The Entire Universe

The entire universe resides within you. Artists know this intrinsically, as do musicians & philosophers and the rest. If you have a problem it is yours, fix it in yourself.

## Contrary to the Obvious

Contrary to the Obvious ~
You are the one who has been hurting you.

## UnDeath

What if you found out that you never die
so you didn't have to avoid death...
How would that affect every decision?

## The Waiting

With feet burning blisters
and fingers blackened bloody
ordained to walk in the winds of the desert
now deaf and dumb
I stand before a mute god
there is nothing to do
but wait.

# Near Death

When I got melanoma 30 years ago & my doctor told me I was going to die. He must have been psychic.

When my motorcycle spun out in rush hour traffic, with books in my left hand & the right hand on the accelerator, a transport truck in front, cars everywhere. As I did an inadvertent wheelie, the front wheel lifted exponentially, then turned due to gravity & the bike accelerated. I blacked out. When I regained consciousness, I was riding along normally.

When I came over a hill on the highway in the rain in my Austin Mini and a car was straddling my lane sideways, waiting to turn into the oncoming lane, a guardrail on the right. I realized if I could knock my mirror off with her tail light, I might live. I simply heard a slight click as they passed.

When I crossed Cootes Paradise in spring breakup with my pal, Jocko, & had to dive on mini ice floes headlong into the icy water for 2 miles.

When I went fishing in the Frobisher River & the ice started crumbling underneath me. I had to lie flat and roll to shore, thereby spreading the weight.

When my car fell into the Credit River just when I was about to catch a trout. It pushed me in the water & I swam like hell so it wouldn't land on me.

When the paving machine I was operating rolled over.
When the earth scraper I was operating rolled over.

*First Person Singular* / Ross Ulysses Munroe

When my Land Rover rolled over in the bush in the winter, with the entire crew in it. They were yelling joyously at me to hit the Boonies. Alberta can be like that.

When we were lighting diesel fires in the Yukon & my partner threw his 5-gallon pail of gasoline on the flames.

When I was chased by a Grizzly Bear down the Yukon Highway for a half-mile to the truck & beat him. Fear will do that - which is faster, the rabbit or the fox? While the fox is running for his dinner, the rabbit is running for his life.

When I was climbing the Hamilton escarpment, and fell.

When I set my parent's basement on fire, full of paint & Varsol, through a miscalculation in thermodynamics.

When I slipped on the ice 100 feet up an oil derrick with no safety harness.

When I was the lead singer in a band & nobody clapped.

When the small plane we were on in Antigua got caught in the air stream of a Jumbo Jet & flipped 90 degrees in one second.

When I flew into Cape Dorset in a blizzard & the pilot tried to land on the runway sideways.

When the 3-ton metal floor of the oil rig fell on me. I heard a small clink & dropped and flattened to the ground within a second, with 12" to spare as it hit the wellhead.

When carjackers attacked me 2 different times & on both occasions I pretended I had a black belt. I did, actually, but it was holding my pants up.

That's when I realized this isn't my life.

.

Manor House / 905-648-4797
www.manor-house-publishing.com